EWAN McGREGOR:

Sexy!
Smart!
Superstar!

People magazine called him "a young actor on the verge of superstardom." British *Cosmopolitan* named him one of the sexiest men in the world. And with his new *Star Wars* role, he may soon be called the sexiest man in the universe! Now you can learn about . . .

- His freewheeling lifestyle, both on and off the movie set

- How he met—and married—the girl of his dreams

- Behind-the-scenes looks at his early career

- His unconventional—and happy—family life

EWAN McGREGOR
Rising to the Stars

James Hatfield

BERKLEY BOULEVARD BOOKS, NEW YORK

EWAN MCGREGOR: RISING TO THE STARS

A Berkley Boulevard Book / published by arrangement with the author

PRINTING HISTORY
Berkley Boulevard edition / May 1999

All rights reserved.
Copyright © 1999 by Omega Publishing Endeavours, Inc.
Book design by Tiffany Kukec.
Cover design by Elaine Groh.
Cover photograph by London Features.
This book may not be reproduced in whole or in part,
by mimeograph or any other means, without permission.
For information address: The Berkley Publishing Group, a
division of Penguin Putnam Inc., 375 Hudson Street,
New York, New York 10014.

The Penguin Putnam Inc. World Wide Web site address is
http://www.penguinputnam.com

ISBN: 0-425-16900-6

BERKLEY BOULEVARD
Berkley Boulevard Books are published by The Berkley
Publishing Group, a division of Penguin Putnam Inc.,
375 Hudson Street, New York, New York 10014.
BERKLEY BOULEVARD and its logo
are trademarks belonging to Penguin Putnam Inc.

PRINTED IN THE UNITED STATES OF AMERICA

10 9 8 7 6 5 4 3 2 1

My heart beats for only one woman—
my wife and best friend, Nancy.
I don't always *tell her,*
but I will always *love her.*
This one is dedicated to you, Red!

And, for George "Doc" Burt,
my coauthor on six books and, more importantly,
a true friend when friends were about as hard
to come by as a glass of water in a desert.
You're a class act, Quardoc!

*"I've been driven all my career,
but I have no idea where I'm going.
I don't even have goals.
But I couldn't have imagined any more of a fairy tale."*

—Ewan McGregor, 1998

CONTENTS

Acknowledgments   xi
Prologue: Full Circle   1

Part One
ALL THE WORLD'S A STAGE

1 Big Screen Dreams   7
2 A Star Is Born   18
3 Nothing to Hide   26
4 From the Grave to the Altar   34
5 Ewanspotting   43
6 A Man of Many Parts   56
7 All in the Family   67
8 Made in America   77

Part Two
ARRIVAL TIME

9   Leading Lady   87
10 Trouble in Paradise   97
11 Extreme Measures   105

12 The Wan and Obi   114
13 Return to a Galaxy Far, Far Away   125
14 Endings and Beginnings   136
15 Onward and Upward   148
16 The Calm Before the Storm   157

Epilogue: Crystal Ball   169
Ewan's Vital Statistics   172
Ewan Fast Facts   175
Ewan in Cyberspace   178
How to Contact Ewan   182
Ewan's Acting Awards   184
Filmography   186
Bibliography   195

ACKNOWLEDGMENTS

(Also Known as "I Couldn't Have Done It Without You")

I'm indebted to so many people who helped make this book possible. First and foremost is my literary agent, Laura Tucker of Richard Curtis Associates, who recognized the potential of this project and had enough faith in my writing skills to pitch me to the major leagues. Thanks, Laura, for selling this one and being so much fun to converse with by E-mail (when you're not off gallivanting around the country, that is). Special pats on the back also go to my editors, Martha Bushko and Barry Neville (although he pulled the rip cord and bailed out on me early), and everyone else who worked on this book at Berkley.

Without running the risk of sounding too melodramatic, this book might never have come into existence without the combined efforts of Alyse Pozzo, Jess Latham, Marie Pier Godère, Eric Larsen, Brian Linder, and, especially my ol' Aggie buddy, Scott Chitwood. I offer this unique group of Ewan McGregor and *Star Wars* fans my sincerest thanks for supplying videotapes of

Ewan's movies and television appearances, invaluable resource material; double-checking my facts; providing behind-the-scenes information on the filming of the first prequel; and for *always* coming forward with enthusiasm on short notice to lend me a helping hand.

I also want to thank those overworked and underpaid "publishing partners" who have always aggressively promoted my previous books: Fayetteville, Arkansas's Jon Dowdy at Hastings; Kris Swim at B. Dalton; Mike Hills at Barnes & Noble; Shannon Smith with Barnes & Noble in Houston, Texas; and, of course, Doug Waterhouse, president of the premiere online sci-fi bookstore, StarBooks.

As always, I'm eternally grateful to horror author and mentor, Ruby Jean Jensen ("over two million copies of her books in print"), who is not only my sounding board for ideas, but one of my dearest friends; Bruce Gabbard, the computer guru who typically comes riding over the hill like some electronic version of the calvary to save me from the one-eyed monster; and Tracy Bernstein, my first editor, comrade in the trenches, and quasitherapist who always listened (or at least had the courtesy to act interested) when an ol' Arkansas boy talked endlessly on the phone about the latest book project. My sincere appreciation for her enthusiasm, encouragement, and never-flagging support during the editing and publication of six books. Live long and prosper, kiddo.

What would an acknowledgments page in one of my books be without my heartfelt thanks to the Beau Terre gang: Colon and Dana Washburn, Karla Mitchell and Dusty White, Mark Levine and his brother Bradley (a New Yorker whose timing is impeccable, usually showing up in Northwest Arkansas just in time for a party), Jeff Smith, Danny and Lena Lewis, Boyd and Deborah Billingsley (*especially* Danny and Boyd—two guys who worked their combined magic to put my wife and me in a new house last year), Daymon and Betty Taylor, Scott and Jane Hundley, Scott and Kelli Eccleston, and of course, last but certainly not least, Chris and Lisa Brooks. Their good company, food, drinks, and cigars always fortify me until the manuscript deadline is met. Of course, let's not forget the young adults (they're *never* kids, of course)—Maegan Washburn, Rachel White and Tiffany Smith—the *real* Spice Girls!

And finally, a die-hard Ewan McGregor fan must be acknowledged—Andrew Alan Bushko, who is extremely proud of his daughter for editing this book. But, of course, he thought she was the apple of his eye when he took her to a Yankees game and she cursed out Cecil Fielder in true Ewan fashion.

Thanks, gang!

Prologue

FULL CIRCLE

"I've been waiting twenty years to have my own light saber. Nothing's cooler than being a Jedi Knight."

—Ewan on the excitement of being
in the *Star Wars* prequels

In 1978, several months after the original *Star Wars* became a blockbuster movie in America and in other parts of the world, the modern-day classic, with its timeless story of good triumphing over evil, finally premiered at the small Odeon theater in Perth, Scotland.

An anxious seven-year-old Ewan McGregor watched the clock all day long at school, counting down the hours. When the bell finally rang, Ewan ran as fast as he could across the playground and impatiently paced back and forth outside the school gates, waiting for his mother to pick him up in the family car.

When she arrived a few minutes later, she drove him the fifteen miles to nearby Perth, where they joined the long line of eager moviegoers outside the theater, most of whom had purchased their tickets weeks in advance.

Once they settled into their seats in the darkened cinema, the audience immediately began to cheer and applaud when they saw the words "A long time ago, in a galaxy far, far away . . ." appear on the big screen. For the next two hours, young Ewan and the crowd were dazzled by the groundbreaking special effects and the exciting story of a young farm boy, Luke Skywalker, who gets caught up in a galactic battle between an evil empire and a small group of rebel fighters struggling to survive. Along the way, Luke has to rescue the captive Princess Leia, deliver the stolen blueprints of the Empire's awesome Death Star space weapon to the rebellion, and stop the ultimate screen villain, the black-clad Darth Vader, partly by using a mysterious power called the Force. Just as Dorothy enlisted the help of the Scarecrow, the Tin Man, and the Cowardly Lion, young Luke meets up with a smuggler and daredevil pilot, Han Solo, and a swashbuckling old Jedi Knight, Obi-Wan Kenobi, who helps the farm boy learn the ways of the Force and against all odds does battle against the Empire.

As most of the audience left the theater, Ewan and his mother stayed behind to watch the credits roll across the screen. Finally, an all-too-familiar name appeared in small letters: "Red Two (Wedge) . . . Dennis Lawson." This is what truly made *Star Wars* a special event for the young Scottish boy. Lawson, who played the only other X-wing pilot besides Luke Skywalker to battle the Empire's dark forces and survive, was Ewan's uncle. Spotting him during the movie, though, had not been an easy task. Not only was Lawson in the film for only a few minutes, but every time he appeared on screen, his face was partially hidden behind a large fighter pilot's helmet, and even worse, he spoke with a strange American accent. Adding insult to injury was the fact that Lawson's first name was misspelled in the credits, with an extra "n" added to Denis.

After the movie ended, Ewan joined a parade through the streets of his hometown, Crieff, to celebrate his uncle's appearance in *Star Wars*. Participants were dressed in costumes of Darth Vader, Princess Leia, the robots Artoo-Detoo and See-Threepio, Luke Skywalker, Obi-Wan Kenobi and other characters from the movie. Leading the procession, of course, was the local celebrity himself, Denis Lawson.

Months after the epic film departed from the Perth movie theater, little Ewan and other boys and girls in the area remained captivated by its enduring appeal. "I did have *Star Wars* sheets and a Chewbacca pillowcase," Ewan reluctantly admitted during a magazine interview years later. The future movie star, along with his brother, Colin, also spent many contented hours playing with the toy action figures and their extendable lightsabers at the house of one of their childhood friends.

Ewan McGregor never could have imagined in his wildest dreams that twenty-one years later, it would be *his* face on new *Star Wars* toys and merchandise, nor that his own daughter would be three years old when she saw her father star as the young Jedi Knight Obi-Wan Kenobi.

Part One

ALL THE WORLD'S A STAGE

"All the world's a stage, and all the men and women merely players. They have their exits and their entrances, and one man in his time plays many parts."

—Shakespeare, *As You Like It*, 2:7

One

BIG SCREEN DREAMS

"I couldn't have imagined it kind of going this well, I don't suppose. But my dreams were all of old Hollywood, my fantasies about acting were like Jimmy Stewart and belonging to a studio and making four movies a year."

—Ewan on his childhood dreams
of becoming a movie star

Ewan's parents, James Charles McGregor and Carol Diane Lawson, were childhood sweethearts who loved books and, more importantly, each other, which eventually led to a church wedding on a hot July day in 1966. Although they were in their twenties, living in a small apartment, and barely paying their bills on school teachers' salaries, James and Carol decided it was time to start a family.

In February 1969, the young struggling couple celebrated the birth of their first son, Colin, and at eight o'clock on the night of March 31, 1971, their second child, Ewan Gordon McGregor, came kicking and screaming onto the stage of life.

Ewan grew up in Crieff, a rural, middle-class town with a population of six thousand that rested on the edge of the Scottish Highlands in the Perthshire hills. Over the years, Crieff had gradually acquired an image as a retirement village where elderly people came to live out the remainder of their lives in peace and quiet. However, the town had not always been so tranquil. Three hundred years earlier, it had served as the battleground for the brutal and bloody exploits of Rob Roy MacGregor and his Scottish clan, and was considered to be one of the most violent towns in Europe. Ironically, Liam Neeson, the world-renowned actor who played Ewan's roguish namesake in the movie *Rob Roy,* would costar with Ewan in the first installment of the *Star Wars* prequels in 1999.

During Ewan's childhood in the 1970s, Crieff was small, safe, and practically free from crime, unlike the city of Glasgow, fifty miles south, which was overrun with gangs and poverty; or the Scottish capital Edinburgh, where heroin addicts overdosed in record numbers and the sharing of dirty needles spread the infection of the devastating AIDS epidemic. Although Crieff with its old-fashioned surroundings was less than an hour's drive away from the problems that plagued the inner cities, young Ewan's only knowledge of violence and drugs came from the newspapers, or from eavesdropping on his parents' conversations outside their bedroom door.

As a child, Ewan was a typical wide-eyed boy with an ever-present smile and natural curiosity. His best friend at the time was a neighbor named Jimmy Kerr. The two spent hours together playing with go-carts and, to their parents' amazement, climbing in and out of simple cardboard boxes, which the boys pretended were crashed spaceships on unexplored faraway planets. Like most friends at that young age, Ewan and Jimmy spent the remainder of their time knocking each other down and wrestling.

On one occasion, however, a temper tantrum led Ewan to run away from home. His mother was so undisturbed by his actions that she actually packed her son a lunch and told him to take the family's pet dog. For an hour Ewan sat on an enormous hill that overlooks Crieff called the Knock, and eventually returned home for afternoon tea after realizing that he had behaved badly toward his mother. "He left because he was fed up with everybody," remembered Carol. "I knew he would go up to the Knock and a friend of ours actually met him when he was up there with the dog, sitting under a tree, looking fed up."

Not long afterwards the McGregor family moved to a more spacious three-bedroom house situated on a tree-lined street. With James McGregor's new position as both physical education teacher and housemaster of a private boarding school, Morrison's Academy, and Carol's job at the state-run Crieff Primary School, the couple decided it was time to relocate from the drab, poor side of town and raise their two boys in more affluent surroundings. Young Ewan finally had his own room with a window that offered a view of a large, backyard garden.

Following in his parents' and several other relatives' footsteps, Ewan and his brother, Colin, maintained the family tradition and attended the local boarding school, Morrison's Academy, where Ewan entered the primary section, or elementary-education level, at the age of five.

Morrison's, which first opened in 1860, had earned a reputation for high standards and very strict discipline. Even in the 1970s, students weren't allowed to talk unless spoken to by a school official; could only walk on the left-hand side of the hallways, risking severe punishment if they dared cross the center line; and faced more extreme consequences if they were caught running in the corridors.

Morrison's Academy was a school for both day attendance and long-term boarding pupils, with most of the student body consisting of children from wealthy Scottish society. Ewan was a day student who arrived in the morning and went home in the evening, but even he had to wear the mandatory school uniform. Ewan absolutely detested the drab outfit, as did most of the other six hundred Morrison's students, and was constantly thankful that unlike the boarding students, he could remove the knee-length navy trousers, the white or gray shirt, the striped blue, maroon and white tie, and the compulsory navy blue blazer when he went home every day.

Although he found it difficult to concentrate in his classes, Ewan's grades during his seven years in the primary section were above average. By the time he entered the secondary school at Morrison's at the age of eleven, his self-confidence and popularity with other students was growing as the charming side of his personality evolved.

A creative boy, he became an accomplished musician, playing drums in the school pipe band and winning a prize for mastering the French horn. However, when the band appeared on the local Scottish TV station, Ewan embarrassed himself when he repeatedly wiped his nose on his sleeve between playing passages from Mozart on his French horn because he thought it "looked cool."

Ewan had a poster of Elvis Presley on his bedroom wall and used to gyrate around the house while lip-syncing to old vinyl records of the king of rock 'n' roll. But when he became a teenager, he changed musical heroes—to Billy Idol. He would spike his hair before going to school and played the songs *White Wedding* and *Rebel Yell* over and over again. Ewan also learned to play the guitar, and was the drummer in a short-lived rock group, Scarlet Pride, with red poster paint in his hair and bandannas knotted around the knees of his black-and-white striped jeans.

It was also around this time that an accident almost cost him his life. Angry that all his friends were away during a long break from school, Ewan raced his bicycle down a steep hill at full speed straight into a busy street. As he lost control, cars and trucks swerved out of the way to avoid hitting the teenager who had seemingly appeared from nowhere before wrecking his bike. As a result, Ewan was hospitalized for a short time while nurses and doctors monitored the effects of a concussion caused by a potentially damaging blow to his head. For weeks afterwards, he jokingly told friends his name was "Bond. James Bond."

While attending school, Ewan did surprisingly little acting in class plays, although in his spare time he and his small group of buddies would entertain themselves for hours on the Knock overlooking Crieff, performing scenes from films like *Grease*. "I was a very good Olivia Newton-John," Ewan has recalled with a laugh. "I don't think there was any touching or kissing involved, you know; we were just kids."

When Ewan wasn't playing with his friends on the Knock, he worked part-time at the local stables, where he shoveled horse manure and watied tables at a nearby hotel. Besides horseback riding, the teenager preferred to spend time alone at the lake, scuba diving and swimming.

An accomplished and impressive singer, Ewan performed solos for the school choir and orchestra, and won a prize for a vocal duet with his brother Colin. In sports, however, Ewan's achievements were limited and he couldn't compete with his older sibling. "Colin was very good athletically, particularly at rugby," their father, James, remembered years later. "But Ewan couldn't match him and I think he always felt they were being compared." Classmates said the boys' father gave Ewan a harder time during physical education classes so that he wouldn't appear to be showing favoritism toward his youngest son.

When Ewan was fifteen, his grades in English, Math and Science were less than satisfactory. He was also beginning to experience the intense pressure of approaching national exams, which, if passed, would provide an entrance to a university education. Adding to the stress were the comparisons with Colin, who was a bright student and an accomplished school athlete.

Soon afterward the usually friendly and fun-loving Ewan became more isolated, restless, and at times mean-spirited. The rebellious young man took to roaming the hills around his town in central Scotland, throwing rocks at girls and launching fireworks at innocent bystanders traveling the roads below. "I wasn't interested in school," Ewan told a film magazine in 1997. "I got into trouble all the time and they kept saying, 'Attitude problem.' I was unaware I had one *because* I had one and it was starting to embarrass my father."

It was common knowledge at the time that Ewan wanted to become an actor like his uncle Denis, but Morrison's typically considered artistic and creative instincts as nothing more than temporary endeavors, something that the students would outgrow. Ewan's acting talent blossomed at early age, when he starred in a church production of the biblical epic of *David and Goliath* when he was just six years old. The boy's parents were worried, however, when Reverend Sandy Tait, the minister of the Crieff South Church and the director of the children's play, called the McGregors and told them there was a problem with their young son and could they come see him as soon as possible. "We wondered what Ewan could have done," said James McGregor. "But we discovered that the minister had found out he [Ewan] couldn't read."

The play used dialogue taken directly from the King James version of the Bible and Ewan's lines as David were substantial. "I said that by the time it came to doing it," remembered his mother, "Ewan would know the lines, and I just read them to him every night and we practiced it at home until we knew it virtually word perfect."

Even at such an early age, Ewan's determination to get things exactly right for an acting performance didn't go unnoticed. Shortly before the only rehearsal, while the other children in the play were being prodded, pushed and cajoled into learning their lines, Reverend Tait discovered Ewan alone in the church practicing his lines. Although Ewan's role as David was quite complicated, he was a huge success. The minister, who had also been an impressive actor as a child, couldn't help but notice that acting was second nature to the boy.

As the years passed, the teenage Ewan enjoyed watching old black-and-white Hollywood movies from the twenties, thirties and forties—especially romances with Jimmy Stewart—on television. Instead of watching sports programs on Saturday like most boys his age, young Ewan spent the day glued to the T.V. set, sometimes watching four films in one sitting. "My lust was for those movies," Ewan later admitted. "I just couldn't see enough of them. On the weekends I'd watch black-and-white movies back to back."

Ewan's biggest acting inspiration, however, was his mother's brother, Denis Lawson, a well-known stage and film actor who had a leading role as the innkeeper in the Scottish film *Local Hero,* but more importantly, appeared in all three of the blockbuster *Star Wars* movies as Luke Skywalker's friend and rebel comrade, X-wing fighter pilot Wedge Antilles. "I remember throughout my childhood in the '70s, Uncle Denis used to drive up from London in a sleek Cadillac to see us and he'd always look really different from other people I knew. I wanted to be different as well. He had flares on and sideburns and beads and a big sheepskin waistcoat, with no shoes and long blond hair, giving people flowers and stuff. Right then I decided to become an actor, and I wouldn't let anyone sway me. He was Hollywood, man, and I wanted in."

Feeling trapped in school, frustrated and disillusioned, Ewan sought the refuge of the make-believe world of the movies. "That's called deep insecurity," he later told *Neon* magazine, "and an incredible desire to be loved and wanted, which is also a lot to do with acting: 'Please like me . . . please, everybody like me.'" Ewan has often confessed how he became depressed during that confusing period in his life, and admitted that he "went off the rails" for a while. "I didn't realize it at the time, but apparently I was."

After a miserable summer break before the start of Ewan's fifth year at Morrison's Academy, teachers attempted to impress on him the importance of good grades and staying in school, but his grades in Math dropped so low that it was decided that he should switch to a typing course instead. He pleaded with his school-teacher parents to allow him to drop out of school and pursue his acting dreams. "I felt I had something to live up to a bit," Ewan later acknowledged, referring to his brother who went on to become a fighter pilot in the Royal Air Force (RAF). "But there was no pressure from anyone. I was just losing interest, desperate to start, to get away. There was never any question of me doing anything else, never, ever. But I never imagined I'd be allowed to leave."

At around the same time, the McGregor family moved to another home, a large one-story bungalow house beside a narrow, secluded valley about ten miles east of Crieff. With the heavy rain beating against the car windows as they returned home one stormy night, Ewan's mother, Carol, turned to her typically despondent and sullen son who was moping in the backseat. "I've spoken to your father," she began, breaking the uncomfortable silence in the car, "and you are going to be an actor. That's what you always wanted to do. You don't need to stay for exams. You are depressed, and you should get out."

Ewan has said in interviews: "She was right, and it was a really brave decision for them to make . . . They didn't make me feel bad about it. They were cool about this crisis and that was a huge relief."

Years later, on February 7, 1997, Ewan returned to visit his old school. He gave a lecture to some of the senior students about his roller-coaster ride to fame as an actor, describing the highs and lows of his childhood dreams, how he got into acting and the film industry in general. He also passed on some valuable acting advice to the cast and crew of the current school production of Mark Twain's classic *Tom Sawyer.*

Ewan found himself the center of everyone's attention, treated like the star he had become, something he had only dreamt of when he had attended the school just a few years earlier. The only words he could use to describe being back at Morrison's were "weird, *really* weird." When asked by some of the students if he regretted "bailing out" so close to completing his education, Ewan told them, "I don't regret it at all, no. What I do regret, however, is not having realized that what you are taught in school is maybe valid. I never really made the connection that what you were being taught was useful in any way. I never thought it was and I was wrong in that respect."

Ewan's decision to abandon his education in favor of pursuing an acting career was a controversial one. Although most of the Crieff townsfolk thought he had truly lost his mind, only a few said anything to him personally.

Even worse, most residents of the small Scottish village believed that Ewan's schoolteacher parents were crazy for allowing him to go off on some wild goose chase. But for a determined Ewan McGregor there was no turning back, and if it was the last thing he ever did in life he would prove to everyone that his parents' faith in him was fully justified.

Two

A STAR IS BORN

"You don't need to worry, babe / I'm not in any pain / but just the thing that stops me going mad / is me going slowly insane."

—Lyrics to "Pocketful of Ticket Stubs," a song
Ewan wrote during a stressful time at
London's Guildhall School of Music and Drama

After Ewan's parents gave him their blessing to quit school at the age of sixteen to follow his dream of becoming an actor, "Suddenly horizons widened into CinemaScope, and within a week I was working backstage at the local repertory theater in Perth," Ewan says, looking back. "I did that for six months, and I learned an awful lot about life and about growing, because I hadn't seen anything before."

Since the age of fourteen, Ewan had been writing and phoning the recently established repertory theater in nearby Perth, begging them for a job without success. With some assistance from his mother, who explained that Ewan had recently dropped out of school and wanted to be an actor more than anything else in life, the theater's director, Joan Knight, finally offered the ambitious boy a job as a stagehand.

At first Ewan pulled ropes backstage while working as a member of the scene-changing crew, a job that paid poorly and involved a great deal of hard, physical labor. Sometimes the group of backstage boys practically lived in the theater for a month during twice-daily performances of plays when productions required an overnight shift to take down the scenery after the evening's final show. But Ewan always tackled even the most boring assignments, such as directing the spotlight on to an actor on stage, with his usual enthusiasm.

"Suddenly I was where I wanted to be and my life went into wide-screen," Ewan has stated about his early years in the acting profession. "I had a ball and the depression lifted. But I was also a real pain in the backside because I was so keen. The people there remember me as a nightmare. I wanted to do everything—this, this, this and this—and they would tell me to shut up."

Ewan certainly made a reputation for himself at the theater as a curious young man who was often seen chatting with actors, directors and the stage crew and repeatedly asking them questions, but his outgoing, friendly behavior ensured that he never rubbed people the wrong way. They knew the hard-working teenager was eager to learn as much as he could and they were happy to accommodate him. Ewan's persistence finally paid off and he was eventually cast in a few small, nonspeaking roles such as the theater's version of the Academy Award–winning film *A Passage to India,* in which he ran around the stage in dark makeup with a turban on his head.

Six months later all his hard work at Perth Repertory Theater paid off when Ewan successfully beat out two hundred other applicants attempting to gain entrance into a one-year drama course at Kirkcaldy (pronounced "Kir-coddy") College of Technology, located in southern Fife, Scotland, on the banks of the River Forth. Although Kirk-caldy was a technical college intended mainly for students who wanted to learn skills in the building trade, the school was known for its outstanding drama course, which attracted would-be actors from all over the country.

In August 1988, at the age of seventeen, Ewan left home in his newly acquired light-green Volkswagen Beetle. Like any other teenager on the verge of adulthood, he was worried about being on his own for the first time in his life without the financial support of his family. "I loved Crieff, but it's the kind of place I eventually wanted to leave," Ewan explained. "That's nothing against the place itself, but there isn't a great acting industry in Crieff, so obviously I had to get out."

At Kirkcaldy, Ewan lived in a tiny dormitory room containing only a single bed, desk, chair, closet, sink and easy chair (he had to share a hall bathroom with five other students), but the limited space didn't really matter because he wasn't in the cramped living quarters very often. Ewan and his fellow drama students typically worked twelve-hour days, producing four stage plays a year, which required them to stay late into the night to meet deadlines.

Hard work, however, was something Ewan had grown accustomed to while at the Perth theater, and the codirector of drama, Lynn Baines, was particularly impressed with the down-to-earth young man who was willing to learn every aspect of the acting profession. "From the minute he walked in the door he was enthusiastic, willing to do anything you threw at him. He was talented and very hard-working."

For almost a year, Ewan and the other drama-school students were put through an intense course designed to provide them with a basic knowledge of all areas of theater, from stage acting to voice control and accents to movement and dance to publicity and promotion. Ewan planned to use the course as a launching pad to admittance into more prestigious drama schools, hopefully one in London.

During his first term at Kirkcaldy, Ewan utilized skills he had learned at Perth and worked as a stage manager for a production, which required him to be responsible for everything from making sure the costumes fit properly to ensuring that stage scenery was in place at the right time. In the second term, Ewan played the part of the conservative music teacher in a performance of *The Prime of Miss Jean Brodie*. During the drama course's third term, he combined a stage-management role with a major part in a parody of Arthur Miller's *A View from the Bridge*. The final production of the year was a play called *Missfoot,* in which Ewan took a minor acting role while once again doing double-duty as the stage manager.

"It was a hard year," he later admitted. "I had to do everything—make the sets, design costumes, publicize the play, act in it, stage manage it. For a young boy it was a lot of responsibility but I learned an awful lot and it was a great stepping stone."

In the course's year-end test, Ewan and classmate Andy Milarvie decided to bypass the usual serious dance routines and selected a slapstick Batman skit instead. With Ewan riding a kid's tricycle outfitted as the Batmobile while dressed in a homemade Caped Crusader costume, and Andy playing his archenemy the Joker, the two students brought the drama class to hysterics as they played the routine out on stage with a backdrop covered in posters that read KERPOW, ZAP and POW. To no one's surprise, the ever-popular and imaginative Ewan was awarded with passing grades for the course.

The drama course at Kirkcaldy ended without any type of formal graduation ceremony and a few days later Ewan rushed off to London, where he applied for admittance into Britain's most prestigious drama school, the Royal Academy of Dramatic Arts. Although Ewan's uncle Denis had written his nephew's audition speech, the young actor was rejected by an uninterested and obviously bored interviewer who believed Ewan was too young to be admitted to the school.

Disappointed and angry that he was passed over due to his age rather than a lack of talent, Ewan journeyed back to Scotland. Shortly after his return, however, the Guildhall School of Music and Drama, one of the country's leading training colleges, granted him an interview. Ewan competed with a hundred other applicants, enduring exhausting and thorough auditions that lasted more than two days. Ewan apparently impressed the staff despite his youth because when they gathered to pick twenty-six successful candidates, Ewan was one of the first to be chosen.

After working as a waiter at a pizzeria to earn extra money to fund his move to London, Ewan took up residence in a small room at a YMCA hostel just a few minutes' away from Guildhall. For a young man who had grown up in a town of only six thousand, living in the crowded capital city of England with a population of seven million came as a real cultural shock to the struggling actor. Ewan phoned home quite often to seek reassurance from his enormously supportive parents.

Although James and Carol lived a comfortable lifestyle in Crieff on their teachers' salaries, and helped out their son financially whenever they could afford it, Ewan was broke most of the time and was forced to sell his beloved Volkswagen Beetle to raise extra cash to pay for his living expenses and three-year vocational courses at Guildhall. He also worked part-time at a variety of jobs, and sang with one of his drama school pals, Zubin Varla, in a vegetarian restaurant on Sundays. They called themselves Mano et Mano.

Just as in Kirkcaldy, the hours were long, often from nine in the morning until seven at night, with dialogue lines from productions to memorize afterwards. However, the training and teaching methods were much more rigorous and challenging than the Scottish drama course, ranging from voice techniques to stage fighting. The Guildhall curriculum encouraged students to open up and express their emotions while the staff examined their acting abilities in microscopic detail, a tough but thorough process that made many would-be actors, including Ewan, realize they weren't as good as they previously believed. At first, Ewan's self-confidence was shattered and he seriously began to doubt if he could ever successfully complete the three years of studies required for graduation.

The enormous pressures placed on the teenage students at the drama school, in addition to being away from home for the first time and in a new city, were just too much for many of them to bear. Robert Carlyle, who would later costar with Ewan in *Trainspotting* and then shoot to fame in the Academy Award–nominated comedy *The Full Monty,* commented in a British newspaper about his time spent as a student at the Royal Academy of Music and Drama: "It took me at least four years to get rid of the garbage they had put in. Drama school is all about compartmentalizing people and turning them into actors in a conveyor belt sort of way. There is a terrible generalization in the way they teach . . . You are analyzing the wrong stuff because you are looking at each other. Life is what you should be looking at."

Eventually, Ewan realized that he wasn't "one of the best actors in the world," and accepted the fact that he had much to learn. It was a difficult process, but he grew to appreciate the training. In addition to performing in a series of small plays during his second year at Guildhall, Ewan toured Europe in a production of *As You Like It,* playing the role of Orlando. "That boosted my confidence quite a lot because I had always been scared of Shakespeare," he later confessed in a newspaper interview. Encouraged to "bare his soul" by the school staff, Ewan's natural talent began to benefit from the strict and disciplined teaching exercises.

Midway through his third and final year, Ewan prepared for the annual showcase in front of two hundred casting directors and agents who could make or break his career. In the middle of his performance about an oil worker who had lost his legs in an accident on a rig, the young actor forgot his lines. While the audience looked on, he paused, then glanced downward as he rubbed the stump of one of his severed legs. He raised his head again, regained his stage composure and continued with the production, although he was sure the damage had been done to what appeared to be a very promising acting career.

To his surprise, however, Ewan was approached after the performance by Lindy King, an agent who said she was interested in talking to him about the possibility of a forthcoming TV role. Instead of playing a minor role in an insignificant production, Ewan was awarded the opportunity to be the star in a major television miniseries.

Three

NOTHING TO HIDE

"There were a lot of nude scenes but I am not embarrassed about taking my clothes off. I find it real easy. To me . . . [it] is like swimming. It feels really comfortable."

—A typical Ewan comment regarding appearing naked numerous times on stage and screen

A few months before he was to graduate from Guildhall, lady luck smiled on Ewan and he achieved what seemed to be the impossible: The unknown drama student was the top billing in celebrated playwright Dennis Potter's new television miniseries, *Lipstick on Your Collar.* The producers were so convinced that the young actor was perfect for the part, Ewan wasn't even required to perform a screen test. Besides, it would have occurred at the same time as his final college production, and they were happy to let him proceed with his drama school commitments instead.

Several of Ewan's classmates and teachers at Guildhall were jealous of his first big part. They had seen other students in the past win secondary and nonspeaking roles in TV shows, but never a lead part as prestigious as Ewan's. Some of them believed he was in *way* over his head, while others were quietly hoping that the cocky, self-assured young man would fall flat on his face, and be forced to come back to the drama school with his tail between his legs. As he flipped through the script for *Lipstick,* Ewan noticed the frequent appearances of his character and his heart began to beat a little faster. Despite his trepidation, however, he knew there was no turning back now. This was an opportunity that most actors only dreamt about, a once-in-a-lifetime chance.

In early March 1992, a few weeks before his drama course was due to finish, Ewan left Guildhall for the last time to begin production on the six-part miniseries, which was scheduled to take seven months to film at Twickenham and Pinewood Studios, and also on location throughout London. *Lipstick on Your Collar* was to be televised the following year on Britain's Channel 4, the third in a series of musical dramas from controversial playwright Dennis Potter, best known for two earlier TV productions, *Pennies from Heaven* and the sexually explicit but critically acclaimed *The Singing Detective.*

Set in the mid-1950s, *Lipstick* is the story of young Private Francis Francis's experiences in a London military intelligence bureau. His friend, Private Mick Hopper, played by Ewan, is a bored Russian translator forced to work in the War Office. An aspiring drummer, Hopper is a rebel with a cause—trying to drive the conservative, no-nonsense senior officers crazy with rock 'n' roll music. As Britain inches closer and closer to conflict with Egypt over the Suez Canal, the meek and mild Francis, who lives in a dreary apartment with his aunt and uncle, develops a crush on his upstairs neighbor, a glamorous woman named Sylvia. Francis soon begins to have fantasies about saving her from her abusive husband, who also happens to be Francis's superior officer in the military intelligence bureau.

Throughout the six one-hour episodes of *Lipstick,* the fantasies are played out in hilarious musical routines as the characters—especially Ewan's Private Hopper—jive, groove, and lip-sync to the latest rock 'n' roll hits such as Elvis's "Don't Be Cruel" or Frankie Vaughan's "Green Door." The final hour of the television miniseries climaxes at a gravesite, where one of the three main characters is dead, a second falls into the open grave, and a third romances the widow—all to the 1950s tune "Sh-Boom!"

With his hair, eyebrows and eyelashes dyed black for the part, Ewan had no problems filming the Elvis musical sequences. "Doing him was extraordinarily easy because I had spent most of my childhood pretending to be Elvis Presley," he admits. "I just suddenly felt like Elvis. It was great!"

On March 31 the cast and crew presented Ewan with a cake in the shape of a guitar to celebrate his twenty-first birthday; but his proudest moment during the filming of the miniseries was when his parents paid a visit to the set. Although Ewan believed that he had surely disappointed them when he had quit school four years earlier, his heart filled with pride when they arrived at Twickenham Studios and Dennis Potter himself treated Ewan and his family to a grand meal.

The actor has mixed memories of the ailing Potter, who suffered from a debilitating skin disease and died a short time later from a painful bout with pancreatic cancer. "He was an embarrassing man to go to restaurants with, very impatient and really rude to waiters," Ewan has said. But Potter had a kinder, gentler side as well. "I'll never forget it. We were doing a scene in a graveyard, and he came and sat down with me. I'd just had my twenty-first birthday on the set," Ewan recalled. "He told me that when this comes out, 'You'll be offered loads of stuff, and you mustn't take the first thing that comes along. Take the things that come from your gut.' And in the middle of this he'd get up, run off, throw up behind a gravestone, and come back. It didn't break his stride. He'd just carry on, a man who had been ill for twenty years of his life."

So great was Ewan's respect and admiration for the man many considered Britain's foremost playwright that he made a brief appearance in Potter's final television production, *Karaoke,* which was made in 1996 after the writer's death from cancer. By that time Ewan had become a movie star, but he wanted to appear in the TV miniseries, if only briefly, as a lasting tribute to the director who had given him his first big break as an actor.

Although Ewan's role as Private Hopper in *Lipstick on Your Collar* was high-profile, he and his other three inexperienced costars Giles Thomas (Francis), Louis Germaine (Sylvia) and Kimberly Huffman (Lisa) were paid barely ten thousand dollars each. But they viewed the television production as a tremendous learning experience, especially Ewan, who had never actually performed in front of cameras.

Ewan watched the first episode when it aired on Sunday, February 21, 1993, from his new bachelor apartment in the Primrose area of London, hoping that critical acclaim and, more importantly, other acting offers would come his way. Unfortunately, generally mixed reviews, low ratings, and controversy surrounding a rape scene at the end of the first episode were the only reactions afforded the new miniseries. In the *London Times,* Lynne Truss complained the lip-syncs failed because they were badly directed, and singled out Ewan's character, Private Hopper, as poorly developed. "We knew nothing about him," she wrote, adding: "But Ewan McGregor was good in the part, and in fact the great all-round success of *Lipstick* is the casting."

Although other critics weren't as kind in their reviews of Ewan's performance, his father was most impressed. "It was funny to see him when he gets up on the desk in a gold suit and does Elvis," James McGregor told one reporter. "I've been seeing him do that since he was a wee boy."

For four months, Ewan auditioned for one role after another, but no one would offer him a part, except for the occasional voice-over for a television commercial. Fearing that his acting career was short-lived and that he would never work again, he became so depressed he found it difficult even to get out of bed some mornings.

Ewan soon discovered, however, that his fears were misplaced. Six months after *Lipstick* aired on TV, he made his motion picture debut as the shipwrecked Portuguese sailor, Alvarez, in *Being Human,* a comical look at the human condition in five eras of history with the main character played, in each case, by Robin Williams, the comedian turned dramatic actor who won an Academy Award in 1997 for his portrayal of a troubled psychiatrist in the Matt Damon–Ben Affleck drama *Good Will Hunting.* Although Ewan only spoke two lines in

Being Human, which turned out to be one of Williams's few box office bombs, the young actor did get to spend a month in the North African country of Morocco to film his scenes.

A few months later, he also landed the role of the page boy Nick in the celebrated stage play *What the Butler Saw* at the Salisbury Playhouse just outside of London. Critics were impressed by his "amusing" performance, especially in the scenes where he teetered and tottered on stage in a pair of high-heeled shoes and appeared fully naked in front of the large theater crowd. "I had to do two streaks across the stage, and I used to quite look forward to it," Ewan later said, acknowledging that he actually felt comfortable performing in the nude. "As soon as I came on, there were gasps, just because there was a naked man on stage. I used to love it . . . This is what they mean by 'the long line of McGregors.'"

Then came the audition for the swashbuckling and handsome hero of an epic new television miniseries, *Scarlet and Black,* a costume drama based on Stendhal's classic nineteenth-century French novel *Le Rouge et Le Noir.* The three episodes were scheduled for a prime-time Sunday-night slot on the British broadcasting network BBC1 later that year and was expected to be watched by millions of viewers.

A week before rehearsals were set to begin, however, Ewan panicked. "I had a complete crisis," he later acknowledged during an interview. "I suddenly felt crushed by the weight of responsibility inherent in the part, and genuinely doubted I was up to it. I was scared. But the final straw was when a fellow actor told me that, bar Hamlet, this had to be the best part for a young actor."

Returning home to Scotland once again to seek encouragement and moral support from his always-supportive parents, Ewan relaxed and his fears were soon eliminated by the time he headed back to the location shoot. "Once I put on my military uniform and we started filming in France everything fell into place," he told a reporter. "The uniform had an amazing effect on me . . . I just felt so powerful in it."

Scarlet and Black's story line centers around the rise and fall of Julien Sorel, Ewan's character, a poor carpenter's son who idolizes the French emperor Napoleon and sets out on a ruthless, ambitious scheme to become wealthy and powerful in Paris society. Along the way, the Don Juan-like Sorel seduces two innocent, unsuspecting women and is eventually beheaded by a guillotine for trying to kill one of his lovers.

The script for the miniseries required Ewan to spend much of his time completely nude during the seven weeks of filming in France. "One day I was naked the whole time," he stated. "We had to film a sequence in four different places so I was just driven about in a dressing gown. At other times I was running around naked, jumping out windows carrying bundles of clothes while being shot at. I quite enjoyed it actually."

In addition to steamy scenes in which he and actress Alice Krige (who later played the Borg Queen in *Star Trek: First Contact*) rolled around nude on the carpet, Ewan also persuaded *Scarlet and Black* director Ben Bolt to let him run through a French field without any clothes on. Although Bolt was concerned that his leading actor might fall on rocks or glass, Ewan would not take no for an answer. "I persuaded him. I went on and on until he agreed," the actor has explained. "And I must say, it was a very nice experience." Although many television and film actors refuse to do nude scenes, Ewan has never been embarrassed about taking off his clothes in front of the camera, as long as the script justifies the nudity.

Although Ewan received mail bags full of fan letters from admiring teenage girls after the miniseries aired on television, the critics weren't so complimentary. Cosmo Landesman wrote in the *London Sunday Times:* "As Julien, Ewan McGregor is simply too soft and too sweet." Joe Steeples of the *Sunday Mirror* added: "The performance by Ewan seemed short on stamina . . . Series like this are costly. No doubt spicy sex helps sell them around the world. But am I alone in missing the days when BBC costume drama was innocent enough for the whole family?" Simon London of the *Daily Mirror* complained that "McGregor could have beefed up his role a bit," and Peter Paterson protested that Ewan was "far too devastatingly handsome a toy-boy for Julien."

An audience of over 10 million viewers, however, spoke much louder than the critics, confirming *Scarlet and Black*'s status as a wildly popular TV miniseries and elevating Ewan's career to new heights. Within days he would receive a telephone call from a director who wanted the new star to audition for the lead in *Shallow Grave,* a major motion picture set in his home country of Scotland.

Four

FROM THE GRAVE
TO THE ALTAR

"I love to see myself up there because I can't believe it's me."

—Ewan describing the excitement of seeing
himself on movie screens

Ewan considered his performance in *Scarlet and Black* "a bit stiff," and thus resolved "to rock back on my heels a bit and be more relaxed" for the audition of *Shallow Grave*'s wisecracking journalist Alex Law.

Although Ewan competed against hundreds of other actors, including the highly respected Robert Carlyle (*Trainspotting, The Full Monty*), he was quickly chosen for the role after reading a few lines of dialogue from the script for the film's production team, which consisted of Andrew Macdonald, an inexperienced film producer; doctor-turned-aspiring-screenwriter John Hodge; and Danny Boyle, a theater and television director who was going behind the cameras for his first major motion picture. The cutting-edge British filmmakers would later produce *Trainspotting* and *A Life Less Ordinary,* two films starring Ewan, plus *The Beach,* teen heartthrob

Leonardo DiCaprio's first acting assignment after the hugely successful *Titanic.*

Shallow Grave, as its title suggests, is a dark and gory thriller along the lines of *Pulp Fiction,* the Quentin Tarantino–directed film starring John Travolta. The movie opens with three roommates played by Ewan, Kerry Fox (*Welcome to Sarajevo*) and Christopher Eccleston (*A Price Above Rubies*) as they conduct interviews to find a fourth prospective tenant for the spare bedroom in their elegant top-floor apartment. Although the trio humiliate every applicant that shows up, a mysterious novelist named Hugo refuses to be ridiculed and is awarded the extra bedroom. Unfortunately, he overdoses on drugs shortly after moving in, and when the curious roommates break his door down, they discover a stark-naked Hugo dead on the bed and a suitcase full of money underneath it. Although the journalist (Ewan), the doctor (Fox) and the accountant (Eccleston) decide to keep the money, they are faced with the problem of what to do with the dead body. A decision is made to dispose of the corpse quickly by cutting it up into several pieces to reduce the chances of identification before burying it in a shallow grave. Soon afterwards, however, Hugo's partners in crime show up looking for the cash, police officers begin asking questions, and the greedy roommates turn on each other.

To prepare for the rude, aggressive side of Alex Law's character, Ewan listened to tapes of various comedians, including the American duo the Jerky Boys. Alex's journalistic background came from spending time in the newsroom of the *Evening Times* in Glasgow, Scotland, where Ewan was surprised by the amount of time spent on the phone and in front of computers. "Alex says he has been there for three years—three years of writing 'Cat Eats Pensioner' stories. I can imagine him being deeply disenchanted with it all," Ewan has said of his role as the cynical reporter in the movie.

Filming finally began on *Shallow Grave* (originally titled *Cruel*) in September 1993. The script had been rewritten well over a dozen times and turned down by several leading directors who believed the movie was too bloody and heartless. Although it only took thirty days to shoot the film, much of its low budget was spent converting an old warehouse in Glasgow into a mock-up of the interior of an upscale apartment in Edinburgh, Scotland, which served as the location of the story. As a result, Macdonald, Boyle and Hodge took equal shares of less than $25,000 in salary, and Ewan and the rest of the cast took even less.

"It's weird to be doing something in my own accent because it makes me feel very naked," Ewan said of his first screen role set in his native Scotland. Even the actor's mother made a cameo appearance at the beginning of the movie as one of the ridiculed, would-be tenants.

"I hope he remembers us in five years' time," Boyle said of Ewan during filming. "When we came to make *Shallow Grave* we had to talk the [financial] backers into accepting him. . . . He's not one of those drop-dead gorgeous Brad Pitt types—but there's something enormously attractive about him, because he's more human."

"Back then all we had to sell was the team approach," Macdonald later said. "Big names were not an option. No one was going to come and see the film because of the cast."

In early 1994, *Shallow Grave* was completed on schedule and while Boyle and Macdonald began postproduction editing, Ewan flew back to London, where he started work on the new British television series, *Kavanagh QC*. During this time his personal life entered a period of dramatic change when he fell in love with and married a Frenchwoman, thus breaking the collective hearts of all his adoring female fans.

Incredibly handsome and outgoing, Ewan had always been very popular with the girls. A serious relationship with one of his Kirkcaldy classmates, Hannah Titley, blossomed into love almost immediately and some students believed that the couple were destined to get married. Ewan loved her deeply, but the acting career he had always dreamt of was ultimately more important and their separation was not strong enough to survive his relocation to London when he began his three-year course at Guildhall School of Music and Drama. Although they originally lived together in England's capital for three months, they mutually decided it was best to go their separate ways; yet they forever remain close friends.

Following his breakup with Hannah, Ewan lived the typical life of a single, handsome, twenty-something young man. There were numerous girlfriends, but nothing too serious until he met Marie Pairis, a petite brunette, while working in France on the set of the *Scarlet and Black* miniseries. The two fell madly in love very quickly and became inseparable, continuing their relationship after filming finished by taking off on a month-long tour of the French Alps on Marie's BMW motorcycle. Although Marie later left her French home to join her boyfriend in London, where she attempted to find work, a hesitant Ewan essentially ended the relationship when he told one interviewer, "I don't envisage marriage and babies with anybody yet."

In September 1994, while on the set of the *Shallow Grave,* Ewan had become decidedly less willing to talk publicly about his private life. In the London *Sunday Mail* newspaper, interviewer Gavin Docherty noted how Ewan "clammed up like a Venus flytrap" on the subject of his love life. "I have no time for women at the moment," he told the reporter. "There's nothing on the card, and I'm quite happy about that."

Since his split with Marie, Ewan had met and dated other young women, but his carefree lifestyle no longer satisfied him. He was ready to settle down and have a family with Eve (pronounced "Ev") Mavrakis, a production designer he had met while he was playing a rapist on the gripping courtroom TV drama *Kavanagh QC.* Eve, like Marie, was a very attractive brunette from France. Asked later why he fell in love with Frenchwomen, Ewan answered with a mischievous smile, "They're difficult. I like difficult women."

Ewan knew from the first day he saw her that he had fallen in "marriage-sized love" with the cultured Eve, a lover of modern art and movies who worked as a translator on Steven Spielberg's epic film *Empire of the Sun.* Fluent in French, English, Mandarin Chinese and Spanish, the fashion-conscious Eve also fell head-over-heels in love with the scruffy actor who combed his hair very seldomly.

Ewan and Eve's wedding was in 1995 at a borrowed

villa in rural France surrounded by fields full of sunflowers. The couple threw a week-long party that climaxed with sixty guests crowding in the local town hall with the mayor, M. Debet, a farmer wearing a colorful and ornamental sash ribbon over his shoulder. The mayor performed the ceremony in French, which meant that Ewan didn't understand most of the marriage vows. He pledged his love by saying "Oui" (French for "yes") and since everyone in attendance laughed, he later joked, "I'm not sure I said that at the right time."

"It was a wonderful wedding, just the way they wanted," Ewan's father, James, told a Scottish newspaper, after he and his family and several other relatives had returned from France. "But he was the most nervous person I have ever seen." The wedding reception, which lasted for a few days after the actual marriage ceremony, was more relaxed, however. "We all cooked for each other at night, drank fine wines in the garden," Ewan has said. "You know how it can become completely out of your hands? Well, it was absolutely what we wanted to do. That's very unusual, when you have a dream, to actually see it totally realized, which our marriage was. It was perfect."

While filming the premiere episode of *Kavanagh QC,* a new British ITV drama series, Ewan and Eve struggled to keep their relationship a secret (even the show's producer only found out afterward). Ewan, always the professional actor, did not want anything to distract from his portrayal of David Armstrong, a university student who takes a summer job working as a builder at the home of a middle-aged, bored housewife who later accuses him of rape.

In the episode "Nothing But the Truth," Ewan's character, Armstrong, is defended by Kavanagh, who is charmed by the young student and fully convinced of his innocence. After Kavanagh secures an acquittal during the trial, he is approached by a young woman who says she too was raped by Armstrong, and the episode ends on a chilling note with Armstrong holding a photograph of Kavanagh's teenage daughter.

After appearing in the *Kavanagh QC* courtroom series, Ewan filmed the BBC comedy-drama, *Doggin' Around,* in which he portrays Tom Clayton, a member of a jazz band. The musical ensemble's aging pianist, Joe Warren, played by American actor Elliott Gould (best known for his portrayal as the original "Trapper John" McIntyre in the motion picture *M*A*S*H* and as Monica's father on the hit NBC series *Friends*) comes to England to play in small, working-class clubs but finds himself pursued by criminals and the police throughout his tour. Although critics gave the TV movie favorable reviews, its late night Sunday airing effectively killed any high ratings.

Much less notable was Ewan's next movie, *Blue Juice,* his final acting project in 1994. Although he had become a well-known actor by that time and had received numerous offers for a variety of television and film roles, he was excited about appearing in a movie that was already being dubbed "*American Graffiti* on surfboards."

In the film, Ewan portrayed cocky yet insecure drug dealer Dean Raymond, one of a trio of London-based friends who unexpectedly visit their surfing buddy just as his relationship with his girlfriend is beginning to fall apart. *Blue Juice* was set in Cornwall, on the polluted, southwest coast of England, and to make matters worse,

it was filmed it October and November, two of the cold-
est months of the year. But Ewan clearly enjoyed making
the movie, which was never released in America: "I had
a great time in Cornwall for ten weeks," he later recalled.
"I've never partied so much in my life."

One night in particular, he and a friend were sitting and
talking and drinking in Ewan's living room when their
driver arrived. Ewan mistakenly believed he had shown
up to join them for a drink, but the driver was there to escort them to the movie set. Ewan and his friend had
stayed up all night, somehow completely forgetting to go
to sleep. Fortunately, Ewan's lowlife, drug-dealing character was wearing sunglasses in the scene that day, which
allowed him to stumble his way through it and hide the
dark circles under his eyes from lack of sleep the night
before.

Although *Blue Juice* was rejected by critics and moviegoers alike (even Ewan said the motion picture was "not
really very good"), the young actor was beginning to get
excited about the advance buzz on *Shallow Grave*. At the
prestigious Cannes Film Festival in the south of France,
where an extra three screenings had to be arranged to accommodate the multitude of actors and filmmakers who
wanted to see the scary, but hilarious thriller, the movie
was quickly earning a reputation as the most eagerly
awaited British film since Hugh Grant's enormously successful *Four Weddings and a Funeral*.

During the next twelve months, *Shallow Grave* became the most profitable British movie of the year as it
played to sold-out theater audiences and won several film
awards along the way in France, Spain, Portugal, Italy

and at Robert Redford's influential Sundance Festival in Utah.

While critics praised the film as "pure moviemaking," whose "ruthlessness and cruel humor" Alfred Hitchock "would have admired," *Shallow Grave*'s suddenly hot production team of Macdonald, Hodge and Boyle turned down huge offers from 20th Century-Fox and Disney to make films with Sharon Stone, Gene Hackman and other big-name American actors.

"Hollywood wants to control individuals, hoping that what it likes about them will rub off on their product," producer Andrew Macdonald later commented. "It's a deal with the devil, and that's why it's for millions." But control over the finished film was more important than cash, and instead of catching the next plane to Los Angeles, Macdonald, Hodge and Boyle were determined to stay together for a more ambitious and risky project— *Trainspotting,* which would be the most profitable film in the world in 1996 and make Ewan McGregor an international star.

Five

EWANSPOTTING

"If someone's constantly telling you, 'Don't do this, don't do that,' especially as a kid, the first thing you want to do is go and do it. It's much more responsible to say, 'It'll make you feel fantastic for a short while, but then it will lead to this, this, and this.'"

—Ewan defending *Trainspotting* against critics who complained that the movie encouraged young people to try drugs

The first scene of *Trainspotting* shows Ewan's character, Mark Renton, running along Princes Street in Edinburgh, Scotland's main shopping thoroughfare, at breakneck speed. A skinny heroin addict with close-cropped hair who shoplifts to support his drug habit, he is being chased by tough-looking security guards. But as he races down the street in a mad dash to save himself, the audience sees a broad grin on his face.

Ewan, who later described getting the role as similar to receiving "a million birthday presents," wasn't required to audition for the part of Renton. As far as Andrew Macdonald and Danny Boyle, the producer and director, respectively, of *Shallow Grave*, were concerned, the role was tailor-made for Ewan. After reviewing a draft of the script while attending Robert Redford's Sundance Film Festival in America ("where the talk is all commerce and no art," Ewan has complained), he couldn't restrain his enthusiasm for the screenplay: "It was the kind of part you don't read very often and it was exactly the part that I personally felt I wanted to play at the time."

Screenwriter John Hodge originally had doubts about Ewan as Renton. "I only found this out recently," the actor later acknowledged, "but he didn't think I was the right guy for the job at all. The other two had to convince him. But he's willing to say I've proved him wrong . . . They're terribly loyal as a team to me and I to them, but the loyalty would stop if I'm not right to play a part, and that's the way it should be."

Ewan was delighted to be reunited with the *Shallow Grave* team. "I was just really looking forward to coming back up to Scotland and seeing everyone again, sort of taking off where we left off."

Trainspotting, a film based on Irvine Welsh's trendy but controversial best-selling book of the same name, chronicles the miserable lives of Renton and his group of unemployed heroin-addict friends in Edinburgh, Scotland. During the months of careful preparation before filming on the movie actually began, Ewan lost twenty-eight pounds and shaved off his beautiful, long hair to look convincing as the likable but self-destructive junkie narrator.

"He was dedicating a year to us," director Boyle noted at the time. "That was the key moment in which he announced he wanted to be an actor of real range and commitment, not just a pretty boy drifting through costume dramas."

Losing weight was not a problem. "That was just something that had to be done," Ewan told one interviewer. "Renton was living a life on heroin, so he wasn't going to be a beefcake. There was almost nothing difficult about the film because I was so prepared for it. I had such a passion for it before we started, and that stayed with me right through the shoot."

To prepare for the role Ewan immediately cut milk, butter and *especially* beer out of his diet. His wife, Eve, cooked special meals, forcing him to lose a massive amount of weight while he was filming Peter Greenaway's erotic fantasy *The Pillow Book* prior to *Trainspotting*. Ewan told friends to watch the movie closely and they would notice how his character was noticeably thinner at the end of *The Pillow Book* than at the beginning.

"It wasn't so hard to lose the weight, because I had a date and a goal in mind," Ewan explained. "But during the filming, it was hard to maintain the weight loss. Like on any film set there were snacks all over the place. So that was tough."

In addition to reading Welsh's novel for the first time, as well as numerous other books on drug addiction, Ewan prepared for the role by observing a group of heroin junkies at a railway station in Luxembourg, where he was completing filming on *The Pillow Book*. "I didn't hang out with them," he has insisted. "I just watched them from a distance. I'd never initiate myself into the group because that would be too embarrassing . . . I got some of my look from them and some physical ideas. For instance, in one of the first scenes I used this particular stooped posture for Renton [Ewan hunches over to demonstrate] which is an exact rip-off of a guy I saw in Luxembourg."

During the two-week rehearsal before filming actually began on *Trainspotting,* Boyle took Ewan and the other young cast members to the Calton Athletic Club in Glasgow, a rehabilitation center for recovering addicts, where they listened to grim and harrowing tales of babies dying because their mothers forgot they had given birth, first-time users getting AIDS, and successful lives wasted after that initial hit of heroin. "I heard this guy Eamon [Doherty], who ended up being our adviser, tell his drugs life story, and it was extraordinary. I'd never heard anything like it," Ewan admitted. "I'd never felt anything like the atmosphere of support in the room: the giving of strength to each other, from these hard men and women, felt almost religious. Hearing how low they'd sunk dispelled any ideas that I maybe had of any glamour involved with the taking of heroin." After the film's release, the Calton Club received a percentage of *Trainspotting*'s profits.

Contrary to persistent rumors, Ewan did not shoot up with heroin to see what it was like, although he originally wanted to experiment with the drug as part of the research for his character. But what about the gruesome close-up shots in the movie that show him injecting himself with syringes of heroin? "It is my arm," he explained, "but molded prosthetically and with a plastic pipe going into a little pool of blood underneath so you can see the pulse." There is also a scene after Renton overdoses in which a nurse gives him an injection of antiopiates to help him recover. "[She] gave me a *real* injection of saline," Ewan later said. "I was lying there and I couldn't react to the needle going in 'cause I was supposed to be in a state of unconsciousness . . . I'd spent four or five weeks pretending to put a needle in my arm, so it was quite a kick to have one in there."

Doherty, the former heroin addict (he started taking drugs at age thirteen) and technical adviser on the film, came on to the set to teach Ewan and the other young actors how to shoot up properly. "There were eight of us sitting at a long table with a spoon, matches and a syringe," Ewan explained. "He showed us how to do it with extraordinary dexterity, using one hand like he was lighting cigarettes, all the while chatting away. Then we each had to cook up a shot and he'd walk up and down the table and give us marks out of 10. We'd hold an orange in our arm, inject it and go, 'Way hey hey!' "

Trainspotting's seven-week film shoot started in May 1995 in Glasgow and later moved to London. "Danny [Boyle] has a very clear idea of how he wants the film to look," Ewan said at the time of filming. "He has a scrapbook filled with photos and images which he shows us so that right from the word 'go' you have a good idea of what quality, texture, he wants the film to have and how he's going to shoot it: lots of very low and very high angles, lots of feet and leg shots. In a certain sense he knows exactly what he wants, but that doesn't mean you have to recreate his imaginings of a scene, he'll let you find yourself."

After another eight weeks of editing, the final product emerged: a hip, stylish, fast-paced, and at times wickedly funny but depressing and angry masterpiece of low-budget filmmaking. Although *Trainspotting*'s ninety minutes contain drugs, violence, sordid death, sex, cursing, thievery, rantings against authority and loud music (featuring some of the biggest names in Britpop and tenchno, such as Oasis, Blur and Pulp), the movie is essentially a story of friendship and betrayal.

Ewan stars as Mark Renton, a twenty-something, self-proclaimed bad guy who spends much of his time getting high as an alternative to a hopeless and boring future in a working-class area of Edinburgh, Scotland. "I chose not to choose life," he says at the beginning of the movie. "I chose something else. And the reasons? There are no reasons. Who needs reasons when you've got heroin." Renton steals money from his mother and TV sets from retirement homes to support his drug habit, and with his scrawny, drug-crazed, so-called friends—the hopeless but likable Spud (Ewen Bremner) and the suave lady's man Sick Boy (Jonny Lee Miller)—spends his days in the pursuit and consumption of heroin. His other two troublemaking buddies are the lovesick Tommy (Kevin McKidd), who tries his hardest not to touch the drug; and Begbie (Robert Carlyle), the violent alcoholic psychopath, who gets his kicks from barhopping, drifting and fighting. When the group isn't high, they're withdrawing; when they're not withdrawing, they're committing crimes to stay high. In the end, *Trainspotting* has an antidrug message, but it presents its case through character studies, rather than lecturing or preaching.

"The characters are full of humanity and humor," Ewan told a reporter. "It's not what you'd imagine to see from a bunch of heroin addicts . . . In a way, the movie's very much like heroin. It lets you laugh and takes you on this trip. Then it doesn't really let you have such a good time anymore."

No scene in *Trainspotting* lasts longer than two minutes. In fact, most of the rapid-fire images last less than thirty seconds. Because everything in the film happens so quickly, it would seem as if characterization would be sacrificed; but just the opposite is true. The erratic, constantly shifting storytelling effectively shows how great the characters' heroin highs are and how pathetically low their drug addiction can be.

"You wanna see the most extreme things," Boyle noted in an interview regarding the film's explicit drug content. "You don't wanna see stuff that most of us will never go near. We wanna see cinema go out there to the farthest reaches and show it at its most extreme."

In one of the movie's most memorable scenes, Ewan's character, Renton, literally wallows in his own filth, when he dives headfirst into the "worst toilet in Scotland" to retrieve two opium suppositories he's just accidentally deposited during a bout of diarrhea. "Oh, God, yes, all the toilet stuff was very bleak," Ewan confessed during numerous interviews to promote the movie. "It's true to say I felt a bit sick that day. That day was like, 'Please can I get off this set, it's disgusting.'"

Although Renton struggles with the consequences of a terrifying overdose, and in graphic detail goes through a series of harrowing hallucinations during an agonizing withdrawal, *Trainspotting* was heavily criticized for glamorizing heroin before it was even released in Britain. Some newspaper reviewers and antidrug groups said it would encourage more young people to try the drug. Unfortunately, at about the same time, Robert Downey Jr.

ran away from a rehab center, as did Stone Temple Pilots' lead singer Scott Weiland (who was later sentenced to a three-year probation); Smashing Pumpkins's keyboard player Jonathan Melvoin overdosed; and Jimmy Chamberlain got drummed out of the same group after being charged with possession of heroin. Even in America, the Republican presidential candidate Bob Dole mentioned the movie while accusing Hollywood of being pro-drugs.

"That's just stupid," Ewan said in response to the controversy. "But neither does it lecture people and just tell them that drugs are bad and that they never do anything for you. We do show why these characters in *Trainspotting* take the drugs in the first place—they enjoy them, they think they're better than sex—but there is a price to pay in the long run. A huge price. We show that too."

The film's screenwriter, John Hodge, who as a doctor personally saw the consequences of drug abuse, defended the movie: "Some people will have you believe that it must be unpleasant and will destroy your life. But I think the truth is closer to the fact that it is pleasant and will destroy your life."

"All the traditional information about heroin is there," added Danny Boyle, the film's director. "It's just used in a form that is going to get people into the cinema rather than repel them. We wanted to be honest about heroin, so the beginning of *Trainspotting* is highly seductive. The dilemma was that we wanted to make an entertaining film about something that is potentially lethal, and this is something that people may find unacceptable."

A cleaned-up stage adaptation of *Trainspotting,* featuring American actors attempting a slight Scottish accent, made its off Broadway debut in New York in November

1998. Although the Irvine Welsh novel had already been adapted for the London stage prior to the controversial film version, the new U.S. adaptation abandoned the stomach-turning sequences in an attempt to make *Trainspotting* more family-oriented for American audiences.

"If you shove it under the carpet, that's when kids find it interesting, and that's when they get into it," said Shirley Manson, lead singer of the alternative band Garbage, whose musical group was the opening act for Smashing Pumpkins when Melvoin's heroin overdose derailed their tour. "I think the more we talk about it, and it's de-glamorized, then we might have a chance of fighting this kind of problem."

Ewan, who was clearly angry at the constant accusations that the movie encouraged drug use, snapped at one interviewer: "I'm sick to death of people saying *Trainspotting* glamorized heroin. I mean, were these idiots watching? It didn't, it's simple as that . . . Five people shooting up heroin is a lot less extreme than blowing someone's face off with a gun, which people are happy to watch."

The movie was also criticized for its billboard ads throughout Britain, which showed Ewan as the soaking and emaciated skinhead Mark Renton, an image that supposedly inspired what the fashion press called the Generation X "heroin chic" and "post-*Trainspotting*" looks— the trend toward using young, skinny models in stylish, dirty clothes and dark-eyed makeup in the pages of *Vogue* magazine and in Calvin Klein advertisements.

"It is sexy, because it represents danger, and a life that most of us wouldn't lead," Ewan has remarked on the popularity of his wet-shirt scene from the movie in which his hands are hooked under his armpits and he's shivering. "People either decided to be frightened of things we don't know about, or excited by them. So on that level it makes sense that it's an attractive look. And I'm wet. It's a wet T-shirt! So that's good. We all like a wet T-shirt, don't we?" Ironically, in February 1997, Ewan was strip-searched in a Chicago airport because his grungy, long-haired look fit the profile of a drug dealer.

"It does worry me that the characters have become heroes, because they shouldn't be held up as role models," said Irvine Welsh, the author of the popular book from which the movie was adapted, and who makes a cameo appearance in the film as a drug dealer. "They should be the reverse . . . The way people respond to these things tells you about the kind of society we live in now."

Despite all the controversy, *Trainspotting* was an extraordinary success. *Empire* magazine called it the movie of the decade and the *Movieolla* website hailed the film as "awesomely acted and brilliant." Even in the United States, a censored version of *Trainspotting* became one of America's most talked about and critically acclaimed movies of the year. *Newsweek* called the film a "masterful waltz on the wild side." The *Los Angles Times* praised Ewan highly and declared "this is a film that creates smiles out of things that can in no way be described as funny." The *New York Times* called it "perversely irresistible" and the *Austin Chronicle* noted that Ewan made his performance in the movie "appear effortless." *USA Today* gave it three and a half out of four stars and Siskel and Ebert presented the film with a coveted two thumbs-up.

Ewan, however, was extremely angry that American censors cut a few seconds from a steamy love scene between him and actress Kelly MacDonald, who plays a schoolgirl named Diane. "It was a sex scene which her character was obviously enjoying. They didn't like the idea of a young girl having enjoyable sex, whereas the shooting-up [of heroin] and violence was acceptable to them. That's crazy to me."

Trainspotting, which cost only $2.5 million to produce, made more than $70 million worldwide. The Hollywood trade magazine *Variety* called it the most profitable film in the world in 1996. In Britain it became the most successful movie of the year, second only to *Four Weddings and a Funeral* on the all-time box-office list. *Trainspotting* also picked up a number of prestigious awards, including an Actor of the Year honor for Ewan from the London Film Critics Circle, and in the United States an Oscar nomination for Hodge's screenplay. Although its subject matter was considered too controversial for official competition at the Cannes Film Festival on the French Riviera, it became the hottest ticket in town, creating standing ovations at each showing. The Rolling Stones's Mick Jagger, and members of the British rock groups Oasis, Blur and Elastica joined Ewan for the first screening of the movie. At a press conference, the young *Trainspotting* star seemed to have little left to say after almost a week of nonstop interviews to promote the film. When pressed for a response, Ewan stated he would have absolutely no objections to working with Uma Thurman, Sharon

Stone, or Madonna, all of whom had expressed a desire to costar with the hot young actor in future movies.

"Here comes Brit star quality, the next generation," hailed Richard Corlis of *Time* magazine. "In Britain he's firmly established as the Next Big Thing," added *Los Angeles Times* film reviewer David Gritten, "the one to follow a series of homegrown actors—Daniel Day-Lewis, Hugh Grant, Ralph Fiennes—all the way to movie stardom."

When *Trainspotting* was released in America, however, Ewan found his new star status something of a burden. Hundreds of television, magazine and newspaper reporters all wanted to know if he'd ever used drugs. "No, no, no, not at all," he repeatedly answered. "Booze, lots of booze, but that's it." Finally, he angrily demanded, "How about we don't talk about *Trainspotting* at all. So no questions whatsoever. Like, none. OK?"

A few months later, after the movie's controversy died down and he performed a voice-over for a hard-hitting, antidrug television advertisement in Scotland, Ewan clearly felt more relaxed when he told an interviewer: "It's a nightmare of a drug and it's a living hell that these people live. I'm so proud of the film because I think we told the truth. I think we showed the way it is."

Despite the professional pitfalls of appearing in a movie about drug addicts, Ewan succeeded in portraying a character with whom the audience could sympathize, even though few people were able to identify with his lifestyle. Just twenty-five years old, four years out of drama school, and shooting his sixth film in fifteen months, Ewan seemed to be moving as fast as Mark Renton down Princes Street during the opening scenes of *Trainspotting*.

At this point in his career, it was hard to see what was going to stop him.

Six

A MAN OF MANY PARTS

"It's very simple to me that to be an actor is to be someone who pretends to be other people and there's no way you will find the same character in two different stories by two different writers. They are all different people and it's my job to play them."

—Ewan explaining his reputation as a "chameleon," an actor who can play a variety of roles

In the glorious aftermath of *Trainspotting*, Ewan began attracting a tremendous amount of attention. His compelling performance in the film had received rave reviews worldwide and suddenly he found himself being compared to other British actors who had gone on to make it big in Hollywood. Even Danny Boyle, who directed Ewan in *Shallow Grave* and *Trainspotting*, predicted the actor would "be the next Gary Oldman [*Air Force One, Lost in Space*] or Daniel Day-Lewis [*The Last of the Mohicans, The Crucible*]. He's going to become an international star."

In between the filming of *Shallow Grave* and *Trainspotting*, Ewan had worked on *The Pillow Book*, a kinky erotic drama from the controversial British director Peter Greenaway, of *Drowning by the Numbers* and

The Cook, The Thief, His Wife, and Her Lover. The Pillow Book was based on a thousand-year-old diary by a Japanese writer named Sei Shonagon, and starred Ewan as a bisexual translator who accidentally kills himself, is buried, exhumed, skinned and turned into a book. The sexually graphic movie was proof that the adventurous and hard-working young actor could disappear into a role, becoming a face that looked familiar but you couldn't quite place. "McGregor shows that he is one of the cinema's boldest, most charming young actors," *Time* magazine declared when *The Pillow Book* was released.

"I really like being an actor," Ewan told the *Irish Times,* "which means that the most exciting part about it for me is that you get to learn about so many different things—and that you get to play all sorts of different people. I would get terribly bored if I was playing the same kind of character all the time."

The low-budget *Pillow Book* was shot entirely on location in Luxembourg, Hong Kong and Japan at the end of 1994 and beginning of 1995. It was Ewan's first experience of working with Greenaway, a perfectionist whose movies were always beautifully filmed but usually just as bizarre and, at times, grotesquely violent. In *The Cook, The Thief, His Wife, and Her Lover,* a woman's paramour was moistened with melted butter, roasted, and then fed to her husband, and in *The Baby of Macon,* a virgin was raped 208 times.

Ewan later fondly recalled his first encounter with Greenaway. "I read for him in several accents and then he said, 'Look, you're going to be totally naked, and we need to be able to shoot anything.' I said, 'That's okay.'

Then he said, 'Would you simulate sex with a woman?' 'Yeah, no problem.' 'Would you simulate sex with a man?' 'Yeah, that's okay.'" Ewan assumed he won the role in the movie because he was the "only guy in London who said 'yes' to all of these questions."

The Pillow Book begins in Kyoto, Japan, in the 1970s, where a struggling writer and calligrapher delicately paints the story of how God "created mankind by molding him into clay" onto his daughter's face and neck as her annual birthday greeting. The young girl, Nagiko (Vivian Wu), is later traumatized when she discovers that her father has been involved in a homosexual relationship with his boss, a greedy publisher, in order to obtain money for his impoverished family. The publisher later forces Nagiko into an arranged, loveless marriage to his nephew but, still obsessed with the face-painting ritual, Nagiko flees Kyoto for Hong Kong, where the fashion model seduces several calligraphers who elaborately paint her whole body in exchange for sex. Her greatest ambition in life is to find a man who is the perfect lover and the perfect calligrapher. When no artist displays sufficient penmanship to satisfy her, Nagiko decides to paint herself, but finally becomes passionately involved in a love affair with Jerome (Ewan), an English translator who convinces her that she should be the pen and not the paper. "Write on me," he offers. "Use me like the pages of a book." Together, they decide to win over a publisher for her writing by sending each chapter of a novel painted on a person's body. Nagiko is horrified to later discover Jerome in bed with another man, the same publisher with whom her father was involved.

Nagiko and Jerome become jealous of each other—she of the publisher, and he because she has turned to writing calligraphy on the bodies of other men. In a last-ditch effort to win Nagiko back, Jerome fakes his own suicide, which accidentally results in his death. The grieving woman writes a beautiful and erotic poem on Jerome's corpse and buries him. However, the publisher exhumes the body and strips off the skin to produce *The Pillow Book of Jerome* from Nagiko's text. In an effort to persuade the publisher to relinquish the book of her lover's skin, the scheming and vengeful woman sends the *Book of the Dead*, written on the body of a sumo wrestler, to the publisher, listing his numerous sins and transgressions. *The Pillow Book of Jerome* is returned to Nagiko and she lays it to rest in the soil of a bonsai tree, before continuing the birthday face-painting tradition—this time on her own baby, Jerome's daughter.

Despite the fact that Ewan has almost no dialogue in *The Pillow Book*, "from the moment I picked up the script and couldn't stop reading it, to the last day of filming, I thought it was a beautiful story," he has said. "I was scared to begin with, but I think you do your most interesting work when you're not sure how it will work out. I'm into that."

Although the movie's plot and dizzying split screens (which sometimes contain three or four moving images on the screen at the same time) were criticized as being too weird and bizarre for most audiences to sit through for over two hours, Ewan and actress Vivian Wu (*The Joy Luck Club, The Last Emperor*) were praised for the their outstanding performances, especially in light of the fact that the film contained hardly any dialogue or costumes. "People say Greenaway treats actors like flowerpots," Ewan stated to a reporter. "It's true he doesn't direct you much but, once I got used to it, there was a wonderful freedom in that. He does these big, long, wide-shots and you get to just act your socks off."

Ewan wasn't wearing any socks in *The Pillow Book,* or for that matter, very much clothing at all. "There's no doubt you're gonna be naked if you do a Peter Greenaway movie," he laughingly later acknowledged. "There's absolutely no doubt about that. It was a story about a young girl's sexuality, and it wouldn't have worked with the clothes on really."

Even off camera, Ewan was seemingly naked most of the time. "Preparing for the calligraphy sequences was the problem. Every day I went into this cold studio [in Luxembourg] and lay on a bed with heaters at each side. I laid on the bed for two hours while they painted my front, and I often fell asleep during it. Then I stood up for two hours while they painted my back, which was less enjoyable and slightly more boring." Still, he has said being the pages of a book "is a beautiful feeling. And you don't feel really naked. It's like wearing clothes."

Although Ewan had appeared nude in other stage, television and movie productions—including *Trainspotting,* in which he gave the audience a glimpse of his private parts—the actor had never previously spent such an excessive amount of time on screen revealing what *Entertainment Weekly* magazine called "his . . . uh, considerable gifts" for all the world to see. In interview after interview, he was repeatedly asked about the shocking frontal nudity he displayed in *The Pillow Book,* but Ewan typically reasserted his relaxed attitude about performing in the buff. "It's all part of the story. I've been naked in almost everything I've been in, really. I have it written into my contract." Later, he added, "Being naked was far more worrisome for everyone else on the set than it was for me, 'cause they're trying not to look. I actually enjoyed it, the truth be told. There was something incredibly powerful about it. Usually you'd get arrested for that sort of thing, but I got paid."

Ewan admitted, however, that performing in the nude or simulating sexual acts with actresses such as Vivian Wu certainly made his wife, Eve, feel uncomfortable. "It's not easy for her to see things like that. I know I wouldn't like watching her boff someone else onscreen. You have to be careful with each other about that kind of thing, because it hurts. Keep it professional, or keep it in your pants—if you've got any on."

Like many honest young men, Ewan was also concerned how his schoolteacher parents would feel when they saw their son in his birthday suit. However, Carol and James sent him a fax stating how much they enjoyed the "beautiful" film. Ewan's father even joked, "I'm glad to see you've inherited one of my major assets."

Ewan's favorite director, Danny Boyle (*Shallow Grave, Trainspotting*), once remarked: "He doesn't try to represent himself without spots, and I don't think he's thinking about that. It's instinct. There's something naughty about Ewan as well. *Very* naughty."

The Pillow Book, released in Britain toward the end

of 1996, attempted to cash in on Ewan's newfound stardom and success that came from his acclaimed performance in *Trainspotting,* but the erotic fantasy understandably showed only a modest profit at the box office. Yet the movie was a critical success and added further to Ewan's ever-increasing fan base throughout the world. "I just so incredibly adore Ewan! He is just utterly fab in every way," Amy, an online fan, posted on an Internet bulletin board. "Every time I see or hear anything about him, my heart just about bursts!" Julie, another adoring fan of the young actor, wrote in the comments section of a McGregor website: "I think Ewan is a very soulful person. He is extremely talented and his sheer screen presence is magic. I shall love him forever."

An excited moviegoing public eagerly awaited the release of his next two projects, *Emma* and *Brassed Off,* both of which had been filmed a year earlier, in the latter half of 1995. After taking a little less than a month off from shooting *Trainspotting* to regain his normal weight with lots of Kentucky Fried Chicken and heavy, dark-brown beer, Ewan was back in England on the set of Douglas McGrath's film adaptation of Jane Austen's novel, *Emma,* starring Gwyneth Paltrow (better known as Brad Pitt's girlfriend at the time) as the matchmaker who can see the perfect love for everyone but herself.

"On the first day of shooting," a breathless and bewildered Ewan recalled at the time, "I was riding horses and wearing a top hat, tails, and gloves. And I realized that three weeks before, I'd been lying on a floor in

Scotland with a skinned head and needles and syringes all around."

Ewan's role in the romantic comedy could hardly have been more different from *Trainspotting*'s Mark Renton. In starched collars and a flowing mane of hair, he played aristocrat Frank Churchill, a suave and debonair but scheming English scoundrel. "People will just hate him," Ewan said during interviews to promote the film, "because he's just so bloody charming, which is really annoying."

Unfortunately, the only annoying thing was Ewan's acting in the movie, which most critics, and even his fans, regarded as his worst performance to date. One British newspaper critic wrote, "McGregor looks more like the man with no neck than a sex symbol cad." When the movie premiered in America, reviewers complained that Ewan was "too vulgar for Frank Churchill" and that *Emma* may have been the only film in which the actor's "invisible touch seems to falter. You can tell he's trying too hard."

Ewan, who is obviously more relaxed in modern roles in which he can wear faded jeans and T-shirts—or no clothes at all—rather than tight-fitting nineteenth-century pants, later agreed that he was fully aware of his poor performance in the movie. "I think the film's all right but I was so crap, I was terrible in it. I didn't believe a word I said." The actor also later confessed that he had never read the Jane Austen novel, concentrated too hard on mastering a "clipped" English accent, and hid under the sofa when he finally watched the movie on videocassette.

It may not have been Ewan's finest hour as an actor,

but *Emma* was a box-office success when it opened in America, serving as the perfect alternative to a summer filled with special-effects blockbusters like *Independence Day,* starring Will Smith. But Ewan was personally disappointed with his performance in the movie. "It's all right to do a bad one," he grudgingly admitted during an interview. "We'll move on."

And he did so immediately. When filming for *Emma* wrapped, Ewan rushed straight to the former mining village of Grimethorpe in Yorkshire, England, the setting for his next movie, *Brassed Off,* which dealt with the effect on local communities as thousands of families were put out of work because of the closure of coal mines. The rest of the cast had already been on the set for a week, including well-known character actor Pete Postlethwaite (*Romeo & Juliet, Amistad*) and Ewan's friend, actress Tara Fitzgerald (*Sirens* and *The Englishman Who Went Up a Hill, But Came Down a Mountain*). Ewan, however, had spent his downtime in a trailer on the set of *Emma,* memorizing the *Brassed Off* script and intently listening to tapes of Yorkshire accents in order to develop his own for his role as Andy, a young coal miner.

The critically acclaimed *Brassed Off* (the British equivalent of the American slang "teed off" or "ticked off") is a factually based, charming *Rocky*-like film set in the late 1980s concerning a group of unemployed coal miners who keep their pride and hope afloat by playing in the prize-winning Grimley Colliery Band, like their fathers and grandfathers before them. The all-male group, men struggling to keep their families and marriages together while the British government slowly closes the coal industry, is thrown off balance a bit when a lovely woman (Tara Fitzgerald) bearing a fluegelhorn enters their ranks. Pete Postlethwaite plays the dignified, noble band leader who is stricken with terminal black-lung disease but intent on keeping his players' spirits alive. Ewan portrays Andy, the youngest and most charismatic coal miner, who plays tenor horn in the band and becomes romantically involved with the lovely Fitzgerald, his childhood sweetheart. She is the first woman ever allowed in the village band, and is secretly employed as a spy for management.

CNN's film critic, Paul Tatara, praised Ewan and Fitzgerald as "wildly appealing actors, attractive while remaining actual human beings, light-hearted while fully registering the plight of these working stiffs."

"It's a lovely film, and I really liked the politics of it," Ewan acknowledged during promotions for *Brassed Off*. "I was relieved to see it still in the finished product. Sometimes, political things like that get watered down. They could've cut all that and bumped up the love story, but they didn't and I was very pleased about that. It was a very hard film to make, mainly because we were filming in a small English town like the one in the script, where the [coal-mining] pit had closed and everyone there had been forgotten about, just left to fester away . . . I was there for seven weeks and at the end I was just so saddened by it all that I was dying to get away."

In 1996, the always-working, ever-prolific Ewan treated his fans to a cinematic buffet of acclaimed films—*Trainspotting, Emma, The Pillow Book* and *Brassed Off,* the latter which became the opening night film of Robert Redford's Sundance Film Festival in Utah. Although Ewan truly believed he had reached the pinnacle of success and happiness that year, the biggest thrill of his life was waiting in the wings—the birth of his daughter, Clara.

Seven

ALL IN THE FAMILY

"I'm just trying to live life the way I want to live it, the way we want to live it. I got married because I fell in love with this woman. I had a baby with her because we wanted to have children."

—Ewan on life's priorities

Although Ewan's wife, Eve, was very successful in her career as a French movie production designer and writer, she desperately wanted to start a family. In the summer of 1995 she became pregnant and in February 1996, gave birth in a London hospital to Clara Mathilde McGregor, a beautiful baby girl Ewan immediately nicknamed his "wee lady."

Clara's entrance into the world was a traumatic experience, especially for her twenty-four-year-old father. "I wasn't prepared to be that frightened," Ewan later admitted, remembering the night when he rushed Eve to the hospital. "I imagined you had to be this rock for your wife and I just got more and more frightened the longer it went on, that something was going to go wrong. In the end she had a Caesarean section and I had to go in there and all I was thinking was 'Oh no, I'm not big enough for this, not quite sure if I can handle this one.'"

Two days later, Ewan brought his wife and new daughter home from the hospital and began calling relatives in the early morning hours to tell them he was a father. "I phoned a lot of people, crying down the phone to my parents (screeching and wailing)," he recalled. "And they were like . . . (screeching and wailing). Lots of crying people. Lots of people asleep as well. (Bleary voice:) 'Oh that's good, that's good.' (Shouting:) 'No, but I just went through this thing.' (Bleary voice:) 'Aye, anyway, I'll speak to you later, it's five in the morning.' "

Although Ewan and his wife had lived in the same first-floor apartment in the upscale district in North London's Primrose Hill since they were married in the summer of 1995, the young couple realized it was too small now for a family of three. With the money he had saved from appearing in some of the highest grossing British films of all time, Ewan paid a reported $2 million for a house on the edge of St. John's Wood in the North London suburb Belsize Park, which was close to where Liam Gallagher of the British rock group Oasis lived. Although Ewan loved to party with the world-famous band ("I've really got a teenage thing about Oasis"), his goal was to have "a big house, so my daughter can have a garden."

The responsibilities of marriage, fatherhood and celebrity, however, didn't curtail his nighttime visits to the nearby SoHo district with its mixture of bars, restaurants and clubs. When Ewan first started going out as a teenager, drinking too much beer and meeting girls, Sunday night used to feel like the end of the party. He dreaded it then and now that he was an adult with a family, he felt exactly the same way. "I'm a married man and have a kid," Ewan has stated, "but I'm certainly not settled down." Always the last guy to leave a party, quite often he staggered home, and woke up the following morning with a hangover.

"It's pretty common knowledge that I spend half of my free time drinking and the other half dealing with my hangovers," he has laughingly acknowledged in interviews. "It's not a lifestyle I recommend, but it's mine . . . I'm drunk so often, they're not big stories anymore, it's just a state of being for me. I've yet to be found in a gutter somewhere. I always get away with it somehow."

Eve, on the other hand, is a homebody. She and baby Clara were often sound asleep when Ewan came home after a night of "hanging out with the Oasis boys" or his other buddies, and were still asleep when he left early the next morning to arrive on the set of his next film. "I like going out and she likes staying home," Ewan has said of his wife. "So there's some balance there. Also a lot of arguments . . . I think differences work out. Maybe people who are the same shouldn't really live together."

Ewan finally took three months off from making back-to-back movies at the beginning of 1997 to spend some quality time with his wife and newborn daughter while their house was being remodeled. But the self-imposed vacation quickly turned into a nightmare when Clara was inflicted for weeks with meningitis, a potentially fatal illness that effects the three membranes that envelop the brain and the spinal chord. Although Clara eventually made a complete recovery, Ewan had one of his first run-ins with Britain's biggest-selling Sunday newspaper during this trying period in his life.

"A *News of the World* journalist turned up on my doorstep asking me questions about my daughter being ill," he angrily recalled, "and he wanted to know about it. He said: 'I want to ask you about Clara,' and I just about took his head off. 'Don't ever call her by her first name!' Some things are really offensive and I don't know why."

In late 1996, because of Eve's film-production design commitments, Ewan spent a week on his own with Clara for the first time at his parents' home in Perthshire, Scotland. Grateful that she was alive, he looked back on the break from making movies as one of the happiest periods in his life, which helped to cement a closer bond between father and daughter. "I don't live the rock 'n' roll life," Ewan has stated. "It's not something I've ever wanted. I'm a married man with a family and I'm completely happy with that. I love Clara to bits.

"People might not like to hear this but Ewan is just a really nice guy," he continued, speaking of himself in the third person. "His ambitions are to do the best he can as an actor, not to become a star. He has never been like that and never will be. He has got pals he gets drunk with, he had girlfriends, then he got married, and now he has a baby. The meningitis thing scared the wits out of him. He would have been totally wrecked had Clara not come through that. Marriage might mean a high level of commitment, but he enjoys the stability that comes with it."

The devoted father readily admits that the birth of his daughter was the best thing that ever happened to him. But Ewan and Eve both realized that his multifilm commitments each year had the potential to ruin their family life. "There's a lot of wrecked marriages in this business and we didn't want ours to be one," the actor says. "So we made a pact to always travel together, which we do."

Eve and Clara travel on location with Ewan to movie

sets, where their company is often written into his acting contracts. "I'm lucky my family comes with me wherever I go," Ewan has admitted. "Traveling takes its toll and we've moved around a lot . . . but I'd go bananas without them." If he is only away for a couple of weeks for location filming, he goes solo ("missing gray old rainy London so much" and "that sense of normality, of going to work and coming home every day"), but on longer shoots the family always travels together.

"I don't see it like I've got my working life and then my home life," the actor said. "I just have my life. It's all the one thing . . . I'm living my life with my family."

When Clara began to utter her first words at sixteen months, she spoke more French (Eve's native language) than English. Although a hyperactive child during the day, when she decided that it was bedtime, she dismissed her parents with a wave and a drowsy, *"Aur Revoir."* Ewan was aware, however, that he needed Eve to teach him to speak French, otherwise in a few years Clara would argue with her father and he would have no idea what she was saying.

Although Eve constantly reads books on child psychology, Ewan prefers the more relaxed approach to child rearing. "I'm much more into the way it is, and the moment, and how it feels, and being," he has stated. "I don't want to understand everything because . . . I don't." His relationship with his wife was conducted on equal terms, with both of them shouldering the responsibilities of raising a child.

"I don't think I have ever seen such a devoted father," claimed Ewan's father James, whose home is filled with family pictures. "He does everything—even changes the nappies. Success hasn't changed him a bit."

"How did fatherhood change you?" an interviewer once asked Ewan.

"In the same way it would change anyone's life when they become a father," he quickly replied.

"And how's that?" asked the reporter.

"Very little sex," Ewan answered, and he wasn't smiling.

During interviews, the actor has been clearly uncomfortable with any questions about his private life with Eve and Clara. He happily poses for publicity photos, but never with his family, and he seldom releases pictures of them to the press. The images that appear in magazines and newspapers are usually photographs taken when the trio have been out in public at a movie premiere or spotted dining at a restaurant. His reluctance to have his family publicly photographed began when a women's magazine wrote that Ewan appeared at the Cannes Film Festival in France to promote *Trainspotting* with his "fashion accessory wife and child."

"I'm private in terms of my family," Ewan later said, obviously disgusted by the magazine article, "and I don't like people sticking their nose into that."

Although he keeps his family off-limits to the media, Ewan always makes himself available for interviews, and most journalists are struck by how friendly, charming and honest the actor is, especially if he shows up unshaven and hungover from partying the night before, which is more often than not. "People will do anything it seems, to be a big movie star," he told one reporter. "I don't understand what that's about. I want to spend my efforts making my life the way it should be, instead of trying to spend my energy getting my life in the media."

Ewan also hates being described as "hip," an "icon" of his generation or, worse, a "sex symbol." "I don't waste my time imagining myself as these things. They are things people can think of you as."

And they certainly do. In the British *Cosmopolitan*'s twenty-fifth anniversary issue, Ewan was named the third sexiest man in the world, only behind George Clooney and Keanu Reeves. He was also voted in a British magazine as Sexiest Dad of the Year, and in *People* magazine's sexiest man alive issue, was compared to Albert Finney, one of the best British actors ever, in a feature than compared stars of today with those of the past. Meanwhile, *Premiere* magazine mentioned Ewan in a year-end issue as someone they can't get enough of, and the young heartthrob was ranked second on E! Online in their "20 Under 30" to watch. According to a recent poll in *Glamour* magazine, Ewan's "cute looks and very Scottish accent" even edged out Leonardo DiCaprio!

"Although there are plenty of nice looking men in the world, I have never seen anyone half as good looking as Ewan and I mean that from the bottom of my heart," Lee, an online fan, posted on one of the many Internet bulletin boards featuring Ewan. "He is extremely sexy with no visible flaws that I can find. His wife is an INCREDIBLY lucky woman! Not only is he good-looking, but he is an incredible actor."

"The thing that surprises my fans about me is that I'm an old married man," Ewan has acknowledged.

Besides family, friends and his acting career, Ewan's other great passion is motorcycles. He used to tool around his London home in a 1978 Motoguzzi Le Mans, and more recently bought a $37,500 Ducati seven-forty-eight. "I imported it from Italy, and it's absolutely stunning," he boasted to reporters like a proud parent. One of his dreams is to own a racing team, and in 1998 he tested a racing cycle at the World Superbike Championship in Brands Hatch, Great Britain. At some point in his life he hopes to ride solo through Europe and Africa, attracted by the idea that no one will recognize the international film star under a helmet. "Who's going to know who I am?"

Ewan's favorite hobby is golf, although he has been known to lose a dozen balls while playing eighteen holes and has no taste for high-society country clubs. When he was a teenager in Scotland, he "used to play a lot on public courses, just for something to do." When he was fourteen years old, the management of a golf course asked him to leave because of his loud cursing. "After every shot I would get real angry, screaming," Ewan has admitted. "Eventually this guy drove up in a tractor and told me I had to leave because the other golfers had been complaining. So I had to walk back in shame with my clubs. I didn't play for a long time after that."

But superstardom has made it difficult for Ewan to ride his motorcycles or play golf in privacy. *Trainspotting*'s distributor, Miramax Films, saturated the market with their seemingly endless supply of advertisements, and in the process made his face easily recognizable to a worldwide audience, ultimately leading to countless offers from Hollywood for Ewan to make movies in America. Although Ewan was most comfortable in offbeat, art-house independent films and preferred to choose roles for their quality rather than the financial rewards that went with them, he knew he had to come to the "movie capital of the world" if he was going to expand his horizons outside of Britain and find new acting challenges. "I'll make films there if they're good scripts," Ewan once stated. "That's all that matters, really . . . What concerns me is the story on the page and the characters in the story. When I read a script it doesn't matter to me where it's being made, who's behind it or what film company is making it. It doesn't matter because what is important is the story."

Although Eve told her husband in no uncertain terms that she would never live anywhere but England, Ewan had her full support in choosing his next film role, even if it was in the United States. They both read and discussed the scripts that came his way, but in the end he made the final choice: *Nightwatch,* his first Hollywood movie, which was being made by Dimension Films, a division of Miramax, the film company that had been involved in a number of Ewan's previous projects, including *Shallow Grave, Trainspotting* and *Emma.*

"When I met with agents in L.A., they would tell me that you had to do two movies for yourself and then two for the business," Ewan complained. "And I thought . . . You do every film because you want to do good work. Because you're interested in making good movies and working with good people. To do a movie for a lot of money, like *Independence Day,* I would never taint my soul with that crap."

The principled actor grew angry in interviews if he was accused of compromising or selling out by embarking for Hollywood. "What I am is an actor, and stardom isn't important to me. Success is what I strive for, not stardom. I just want to be as good as I can . . . Filmmaking comes down to writing, and the American film industry seems to have lost the ability to produce good scripts. It's such a huge industry in America—there are films made there that cost $200 million, which is a disgrace. Think what $200 million could do in the world, and they're making a movie with it. It's sick, and anyone involved with that kind of filmmaking should be ashamed of themselves."

The future Obi-Wan Kenobi of the multimillion-dollar *Star Wars* prequels never would have imagined that he would regret what he'd said only a few months later.

Eight

MADE IN AMERICA

"I didn't go to L.A. thinking, 'I've arrived and I'm going to become a Hollywood movie star.' I don't particularly want to be one."

—Ewan discussing *Nightwatch*, his first American movie

Shortly after the birth of his daughter in 1996, Ewan flew to Los Angeles to begin filming the creepy horror thriller *Nightwatch*. "It was my first American movie. It's a bit like *Shallow Grave*, the movie that first gave me exposure in America," explained the Scottish actor. "I went to L.A. to make *Nightwatch* because I wanted to have the kind of exposure that would allow me to pick and choose my films. You can't do that if you just make little independent British films."

In the psycho-thriller being made by Dimension Films, the company responsible for the hugely successful *Scream* movies, Ewan was cast as Martin Belos, a law school student who takes a job as a nighttime security guard at the city morgue. Soon afterwards, he becomes the prime suspect in the mutilation murders of several prostitutes. Ewan's costars included well-known Hollywood actors Nick Nolte, as the detective hunting the real serial killer; Patricia Arquette as Belos's girlfriend and possible next victim; and Josh Brolin as his mildly psychotic best friend.

"It was great to work with Nick Nolte and Patricia Arquette. They're lovely people," Ewan said at the time. "It's funny, Patricia plays my girlfriend in the story, but we had very little to do with each other. We shot most of our scenes in the first week, and then we'd bump into each other now and again. But it was great fun."

Arquette, the wife of movie star Nicholas Cage (*City of Angels, Con Air*), later told Jay Leno on *The Tonight Show* that she swallowed several cloves of raw garlic and persuaded Ewan to do the same before filming their kissing scenes in *Nightwatch,* in an attempt to ward off any passionate thoughts between the two when they locked lips in the movie's love scenes. However, the bad-breath-inducing garlic didn't stop Arquette's and Ewan's scenes from getting hot—hot in the belly, that is. "Ewan's allergic to raw garlic," which caused his stomach to feel like it was "burning," the actress explained to the talk-show host.

Nightwatch, which took only two months to film, was a $10 million English-language remake of the Danish suspense thriller *Nattevagten,* a hit overseas. The new version, like the original, was directed by Ole Bornedal, and featured a hip, alternative-rock sound track (Chemical Brothers, REM). But when the film was finally released in America in April 1998 after numerous delays ("I think they're waiting for one of my really good movies to come out," Ewan assumed), the movie critics sharpened their knives much like the serial killer in the film who had a fondness for cutting out the eyes of his victims.

Entertainment Weekly magazine graded it a D+ and declared *Nightwatch* a "horror for reasons that have nothing to do with suspenseful movie-making. The film students in *Scream 2* would have a fine time doing it in." Mr. Showbiz scathingly wrote, "Note to Ewan Mc-Gregor: get a new agent. The Scottish heartthrob dazzled American audiences with his kinetic turn as a desperate heroin addict in *Trainspotting,* but then he's wasted his time in dismal romantic comedies and now this repellent piece of art-house horror." Mr. Showbiz also added: "Arquette's blonde bangs easily upstage her comatose performance as [Ewan's] bland love interest. But certainly the worst acting here comes from Nick Nolte, as an old, overworked police detective who looks like he could use new skin." Another reviewer described the cast's performances as "terrible across the board," adding: "Maybe it's a great film in Denmark, but it's a terrible, terrible movie in America." According to G. Allen Johnson of the *San Francisco Examiner,* "Ole Borendal, in remaking his own European art-house hit, presents us with pretty pictures and one of the most boring lead characters in quite a long time. And considering the lead is played by Ewan McGregor, the hot Scottish import . . . that's quite an achievement." Although CNN's reviewer Paul Clinton awarded Ewan a B+ for his adoption of a "pretty fair" American accent, he gave the actor a failing grade "for skin care. I'm sorry, but on a forty-foot screen it's impossible to ignore two huge zits on his forehead that keep changing position in every shot."

Ewan, who took the brutal reviews of his first American film personally, grew even more suspicious of Hollywood, where it seemed that the most important thing to movie executives was making money. "I don't like the way the business is run," he has stated in several interviews. "It's not about anything that I'm involved in really. It's not the actors, or the people of L.A., they're all very nice people. But the people who run the business there, executives and studios I'm talking about really. There are as many good American independent filmmakers as there are anywhere else. But the studio system is so lost, I think, and the films that are being made from them are, on the whole, really dire. I speak to the people there, and they don't get it. They talk about A-lists and B-lists in casting. Who cares? They don't get it, so I'm certainly not going to make any effort to crack in. I'm quite happy where I am, doing what I'm doing." Ironically, *Buzz* magazine included Ewan in their top one hundred coolest people in Los Angeles issue, listing him as one of the "Cool as a Cucumber" men, especially considering the fact that the actor absolutely hates the film capital.

Before Ewan began filming *Nightwatch,* he told one interviewer how he believed that his acting talents had played absolutely no part in the fact that he was chosen for the lead role in the movie. In Ewan's opinion, the filmmakers wanted him "so they can put on their poster, 'Ewan McGregor from *Shallow Grave*'," he said. "You do wonder how much of it is about me. And I know I should grow up about it, really. But I've done so many meetings over there where they've said, 'Of course, we want a big American name for this part.' Well, I've got a big Scottish name." And the producers agreed, touting

Ewan as the heir apparent to Sean Connery, whom many in Hollywood consider the biggest actor to come out of Scotland. As one American producer told the *London Times,* "[Ewan's] totally hot. He really has a shot and he's young."

"[Ewan's] the biggest and best Scottish import since myself, of course," Sean Connery himself was quoted as saying at the time.

"It's all there for him, if he wants it," said *Brassed Off* director Mark Herman. "[But] I hope he stays in [England]. He seems to think the work is over here, which is good to see. It's about time somebody stayed."

As soon as director Borendal called it a "wrap" on the *Nightwatch* production, Ewan, who was homesick for his wife and newborn daughter, jumped on a plane to England, eager to leave Los Angeles, "a place which will destroy you, because it's full of liars and flatterers. They will flatter you to death."

Ewan's first acting project after returning home was set in the village of Sixmilebridge in County Clare, Ireland, for a sixty-day film shoot on the $13 million period drama *The Serpent's Kiss.* The rest of the cast was certainly impressive, including Pete Postlethwaite (who costarred with Ewan in *Brassed Off*), Greta Scacchi (*Emma* and the NBC miniseries, *The Odyssey*), and Richard E. Grant (Clifford in *Spice World*). The director of the movie, Philippe Rousselot, had won an Academy Award for his cinematography in the Brad Pitt movie *A River Runs Through It,* and producer Robert Jones was a veteran of the Oscar-winning *The Usual Suspects.*

Ewan, who was offered other, more lucrative films, had agreed to take the lead role after reading the screenplay nine months earlier. "I'm passionate about this script," he told interviewers during production of the movie. "It's one of the best I've read in a long time and it's beautifully written."

Director Rousselot acknowledged at the time of the film's production: "Ewan is an incredible actor. He looks great and he's perfect for the role. He was the first to be cast." Producer Robert Jones also was quoted as saying: "Ewan is a joy to work with. He's incredibly focused and a very genuine guy . . . Everybody wants to work with him."

The Serpent's Kiss, which had its world premiere at the prestigious Cannes Film Festival (as have most of Ewan's movies), is set in Gloucestershire, England, in 1699. Ewan plays a Dutch landscape gardener, Meneer Chrome, who is hired by pompous, recently wealthy factory owner Thomas Smithers (Postlethwaite) to design and build a garden for his bored wife, Juliana (Scacchi). As if torn from the pages of a soap-opera script, Juliana falls in love with Chrome, who in turn becomes romantically involved with her daughter. Juliana's troublemaking cousin arrives on the scene and the plot thickens even more as she eventually blackmails Chrome.

During the summer of 1996, the film crew practically took over the small Irish village of Sixmilebridge, and cast members were often found in the evenings at Paddy Casey's, the local bar, still dressed in their seventeenth-century costumes. Noticeably absent, however, was the typically party-going, hard-drinking Ewan, who instead often sat on a balcony outside his hotel after hours with his wife and daughter, enjoying their company after having been gone for two months while filming *Nightwatch* in the United States.

During *The Serpent's Kiss* shoot, costar Richard E. Grant commented on the phenomenal interest surrounding Ewan: "[He is] astonishingly grounded. Considering the career tornado around him, it's amazing his head doesn't turn 360 degrees."

Ewan's father, James, observed of his son during the movie's production: "His mum and I have been on the set of most of his films and the comment we always get is how nice he is," the senior McGregor said at the time. "It doesn't matter if you're the guy who makes the tea or the director, Ewan chats and makes friends with everybody."

At the end of the summer of 1996 Ewan returned to Eastbourne in southern England to begin work on his next project, which he described in an interview as a "weird loyalty thing": a five-night shoot for a short film, *Swimming with the Fishes,* which is a tale of sexual intrigue directed by his friend Justin Chadwick, whom he had previously worked with in 1993 on *Family Style.* *Family Style* was an eleven-minute black-and-white short film in which Ewan had played a teenager coming to terms with tremendous grief. Although the film was only a few minutes long, Ewan had been pleased to be a part of it as it was during a period in his acting career when he was still struggling to make a name for himself. Now it was time to return the favor and help out a friend in need.

After completing *Swimming with the Fishes* Ewan was looking forward to a well-deserved two-day break between films with his family before heading off to America once again for his next major movie project; but the filmmakers of *Nightwatch* called him back to Los Angeles to reshoot several scenes. Although Ewan cursed the movie's production team and called them every derogatory word he could conceivably think of during a magazine interview at the time, Ewan put the problems with the *Nightwatch* shoot behind him as he looked forward to reuniting with Danny Boyle (director), Andrew Macdonald (producer) and John Hodge (screenwriter) for their third movie together: a romantic comedy costarring Cameron Diaz, entitled *A Life Less Ordinary,* which certainly didn't describe Ewan's rather extraordinary career to date.

Part Two

ARRIVAL TIME

"Lord we know what we are, but know not what we may be."

—Shakespeare, *Hamlet*, 4:5

Nine

LEADING LADY

"I don't think there'd be any objection from me."

—Ewan's response to Cameron Diaz's request
for the actor to sleep in the chest at the foot
of her bed twenty-four hours a day

In the wake of *Trainspotting*'s huge international success, director Danny Boyle was offered several opportunities to make major motion pictures in Hollywood. After meeting actress Sigourney Weaver, the British filmmaker was asked by 20th Century-Fox to make the big-budget *Alien Resurrection*, the fourth installment in the science-fiction movie series. Boyle was even offered $850,000, a tremendous amount of money for a first-time Hollywood director.

Despite a love for big-screen productions like the Bruce Willis *Die Hard* action films and Tom Hanks's *Forrest Gump*, Boyle declined the opportunity to direct *Alien Resurrection*, partly because he didn't like the idea of spending months working on the big special effects required for the movie, but mainly because the offer didn't include his creative team of producer Andrew Macdonald and writer John Hodge.

"Hollywood is a snakepit and we realized that the best strategy for not getting eaten up by it was to stick together," Macdonald later explained. "It's not like we don't want to work in Hollywood, but I do think there is an area somewhere between art and commerce where we'd like to be."

Determined to maintain total control of their projects but interested in doing something light and fun, Macdonald continued, "we developed a story about two people from different parts of the world who are irrevocably changed by being thrown together."

Based upon a script by John Hodge and originally titled *A Life Less Usual,* it was basically a road movie set in France and Scotland. After Hodge rewrote the script eighteen times, the title was changed to *A Life Less Ordinary,* and the story's setting was moved to America.

"Hopefully, it'll have some of the ferocity of the other two films [*Shallow Grave* and *Trainspotting*]," Boyle told reporters. "Only this time, it'll be love that we're demolishing, rather than the human body."

The plot of the romantic comedy centers on Robert, a good-hearted aspiring writer, who loses his girlfriend, his job as a janitor and his apartment within a day. Out of desperation he kidnaps Celine, the horribly spoiled daughter of his former employer's millionaire president. Unfortunately, Robert proves himself a rather incompetent kidnapper and Celine, a veteran of abductions, begins to take over the operation. A cut of the ransom money and a chance at revenge on her cold-hearted father convinces Celine that the situation has potential benefits, leading to a working relationship between the kidnapper and his victim. In heaven, Chief Gabriel (acting on orders from the top) dispatches a pair of foul-mouthed and heavily armed angels, O'Reilly and Jackson, to earth to make sure the snobby Celine and bumbling Robert fall in love and marry. If they fail, the angels will not be allowed to return to heaven. This threat prompts the heavenly messengers to throw danger, diversion, tricks—any means possible—to create a love match between the kidnapper and the kidnapped and drive them into one another's arms. In truth, Celine has everything but love and Robert has nothing but his dreams.

Surprisingly, the same 20th Century-Fox executives who originally offered Boyle the opportunity to direct *Alien Resurrection* were now willing to finance his new film's $12 million budget and agreed not to interfere with the making of *A Life Less Ordinary*. "We sent them the script, told them Danny was director, no questions asked," Macdonald recalled. "They had no rights over casting and couldn't even see the film until we delivered it to them."

When Boyle and Macdonald went to the United States to begin preproduction in July 1996, Ewan was still in Ireland filming *The Serpent's Kiss*. Originally, Macdonald had considered North Carolina for the shoot, but the weather was "too foggy" during their visit. Interpreting it as a bad sign, they changed the film's location to scenic Utah with its vast plateaus and lofty mountain ranges.

Casting actors for roles in *A Life Less Ordinary* went as originally planned, however. "There was a lot of nonsense talked about Brad Pitt wanting to be in the picture," Macdonald remembered. "We met him and he was a super guy, but it wouldn't have mattered who it was, it was written for Ewan." However, Ewan wasn't told, until the movie's premiere over a year later that Boyle, Macdonald and Hodge had specifically developed the lead role with Ewan in mind. "They're so weird, all three of them," he responded after learning the truth. "They don't tell me anything."

The next question to arise was whether Ewan's character should be Scottish even though the movie was exclusively set in America. According to the actor, the *Trainspotting* trio drove him to the point where he almost pulled his hair out. "I was doing *Nightwatch* in L.A. at the time," Ewan said later. "I arranged for them to see five or six scenes from the movie where I was playing an American. I knew that they were watching the scenes, so I expected a call in the next couple of hours. At this point I didn't know if I had the part or not, and I kind of felt that it rested on my American accent. And the call didn't come that night or the next day, and it was about two days later Andrew [Macdonald] called. 'How are you doing?' 'Fine, how are you? What do you think?' He said, 'Well, we just know you too well.' And my heart went blumph. And then I went, 'OK, well, thanks, Andrew, thanks.' And he said, 'Oh, no, we still want you to do it, but maybe you should just be Scottish.'"

Boyle and MacDonald judged Ewan's effort at an American accent in *Nightwatch* to be a major disappointment, as did several film critics when they reviewed the film. According to Mick LaSalle of the *San Francisco Chronicle,* "McGregor's American accent wobbles in and out, but it's amusing to watch the British struggle with that for a change." *USA Today*'s Susan Wloszczyna commented that Ewan battled his "Scottish brogue" and lost. Another critic was even crueler, noting that Ewan "had to use every ounce of his limited talent just trying to suppress his accent, and he did a terrible job of it."

Boyle later explained during an interview why they didn't ask Ewan to use an American accent. "We wanted him to play somebody lost in America, without any family. And because he's Scottish rather than British, hopefully you evoke on some subconscious level Sean Connery rather than Hugh Grant."

Even if the *Trainspotting* team hadn't written the leading role of *A Life Less Ordinary* for Ewan, the young actor later admitted that he still would have been interested in the part because of the film's screenplay. "Reading this script . . . wasn't the same experience as reading *Trainspotting,* because *Trainspotting* truly blew me away," he said. "In this one, the bones of the storyline are more understood. You meet a girl, you fall in love with her, you lose her and then you get her back."

Highly respected actors like Ian Holm, Holly Hunter, Delroy Lindo, Stanley Shalhoub, Stanley Tucci and Dan Hedaya also signed up as cast members. Even Sean Connery, movie legend and former cinematic James Bond, was offered a cameo role as God, but had to decline because of a conflict with other film commitments, although he took the time to tell Macdonald how much he enjoyed *Trainspotting.*

The most difficult role to cast in *A Life Less Ordinary,* however, was that of the movie's leading female character, the young kidnap victim, Celine. Five of America's top actresses were screen-tested before Boyle sent the script to Cameron Diaz, who had costarred with Jim Carrey in the 1994 blockbuster *The Mask* before making a name for herself opposite Julia Roberts in *My Best*

Friend's Wedding, and starring in 1998's most unantici-
pated summer hit, the side-splitting *There's Something
About Mary.* The following day she flew from Chicago to
Los Angeles to meet *A Life Less Ordinary*'s director.

"As soon as she walked into the room I knew she was
right," remembered Boyle. "She was unlike any of the
other actresses I had met; very natural, very fun-loving and
with a great sense of humor, a peculiarly un-American
sense of humor. I knew she would get on with Ewan like
a house on fire."

Boyle excused himself from the blond bombshell for
a moment to speak to his partners, Macdonald and
Hodge, on the telephone. "We've got to offer it to her.
Now!" he screamed. Although they believed casting her
in the female lead role was a gamble, they agreed with
Boyle and the director returned to the room to offer
Diaz the part.

Explaining her character as "a girl who has a troubled
relationship with her father and is a total control freak,"
Diaz told reporters: "The thing that intrigued me about
her is that I'm not that way at all. *Trainspotting* was such
inventive filmmaking and I love the British sense of
humor," she added, offering further explanation of her
decision to do the film. "And Danny's [the director] a real
good actor, too—he'd kill me if he heard me say that, but
it's true. When I first read with him, all of a sudden he
started yelling at me. At first I was thinking, what's
wrong with this guy? Then I realized he was reading the
scene with me and was acting."

Ewan didn't find out until the movie was completed
that Diaz was only one of six actresses who were tested
for the role of his costar. "I didn't know that," he later ad-

mitted during an interview. "But I didn't [screen] test with anybody. I didn't know the chemistry would be there between us, but it was, luckily. Because from day one, it was obvious that we were going to have a good time. And I think because we were having such a good time, you can see it on the screen. You can see in our eyes that we're genuinely enjoying each other's company. It heightens all the romance and it heightens all the fun scenes. There were bits that couldn't go in the film because we couldn't stop laughing. She's a brilliant woman and a lovely lady, Cameron."

It turned out that Boyle was right about his new leading lady and his leading man. When Ewan and Diaz met at the first rehearsal, they hit it off immediately and within minutes were singing and dancing together. "I knew within about two seconds that we were going to have a great time," the actor has acknowledged. "It wouldn't have been as good of a film with anyone else. They wanted a big name, a famous Hollywood actress and they picked the best . . . She's just kind of cool and warm and friendly. She didn't come with any of that Hollywood baggage, none of that movie star attitude that would've made things pretty difficult."

"Immediately, Ewan and I just fit," Cameron has admitted. "We went straight to dance rehearsal for four days. So we got very close, very fast."

"Yeah, it was the drugs we were taking: weird chemicals," Ewan said jokingly to reporters. "No, we just hit it off. It would have been a nightmare if we hadn't. All that romance stuff was *so* there, and our eyes were just twinkling away at each other. It would have been impossible to create that with someone you didn't like."

As part of the research for *A Life Less Ordinary,* the two stars were left alone in Salt Lake City's Tower Theater for a special screening of one of Ewan's favorite classic movies, Frank Capra's romantic comedy *It Happened One Night,* starring Clark Gable and Claudette Colbert. "I grew up on such films," Ewan said at the time, "and that bang-bang, quick-fire dialogue . . . set the pace. Cameron and I had the same kind of tennis match dialogue to get the rhythm level right."

Boyle believed that such research was necessary for roles in which Ewan played "quite a feminine part" in which his character issued ransom demands with "please" and "thank you" attached, and Diaz, the female lead, had "a rather tough, no-nonsense bearing. It's a different stance for the world's biggest, evolving movie star. This is not a John Wayne role."

On screen, the unique chemistry between Diaz and Ewan was obvious, but off screen their friendship was also very close. On the movie set in Utah, they shared a trailer separated only by a partition down the middle. Ewan has told how they often talked to each other in the morning through the screened wall while sitting on their own commodes, or watched numerous videos of old 1930s and '40s romantic classics while waiting to be called to film their scenes.

"All the girls have been coming up to him and saying, 'Ewan McGregor, we're in love with you,'" Diaz was quoted as saying at the time of filming. 'You're married and have a baby, it's not fair.' He has a fun, sophomoric sense of humor—we joke on the set about having gas. And he makes acting seem so easy . . . He's so damn cute. He's charming and funny and, you know, all those things that all the girls want. He's just got it."

Naturally, the tabloid newspapers, especially the British press, began to speculate just how close the young Scottish actor and his American leading lady really were. Ewan encouraged rumors when he remarked in various interviews, "It's very nice to kiss Cameron Diaz, but it doesn't give me any concern about when I get home to my wife because it's work. It's not work of course kissing Cameron Diaz, but I'd like to tell you that it is."

According to interviewer Chris Heath, writing in the British movie magazine *Neon,* Ewan told him: "Let's talk about [the movie], so long as we can stress how . . . great Cameron Diaz is. She's the best."

Diaz returned the favor in separate interviews to publicize *A Life Less Ordinary.* "In the film I fall in love with Ewan's character," she said. "And you can see how any girl could fall for him in real life, too. I loved Ewan's Scottish accent. He has sex appeal and he is going places. The Americans have already started asking who he is and that's the first sign of fame. He is an amazing guy, but he is married."

Charles Grant, writing for *The Face,* described meeting the two young film stars: "Within minutes they've turned into the equivalent of a young married couple, finishing off each other's sentences . . . almost continuous laughter and low-level flirting (if it wasn't for Ewan and Cameron being so avowedly in love with their respective partners, I'd suspect something)."

Boyle admitted that 20th Century-Fox executives wanted Ewan and Diaz to "kiss every ten minutes" in the movie. "We tried to make something more mainstream, but when you watch *My Best Friend's Wedding,* you realize that's mainstream," the director of *A Life Less Ordinary* stated.

Asked by another interviewer if there were any sex scenes in the movie, Ewan replied with a "devilish grin": "There's lots of sex if you look deep enough, baby. It's all in their eyes. We rehearsed a lot of sex scenes, but we didn't shoot them. We did them out of work time . . . we were practicing."

Boyle added that the dance number at the seedy karaoke bar where Ewan sings a rendition of the Bobby Darin song *Beyond the Sea* in the middle of the movie "is the sex scene. This is supposed to be some kind of romance. We can't do a sex scene . . . It just didn't seem right for this particular kind of film, so we thought we'll have this dance instead, which is a very old-fashioned way."

Always eager to have the last word, Ewan has said that the scene *after* the karaoke night is as sexy as this film was going to get: "I've never seen anything quite so sexy as Cameron Diaz not wearing any trousers walking down the staircase. That's about as much sex as you could want in a movie, I would have thought."

Ten

TROUBLE IN PARADISE

*"I'm worried about being shot by the Utah militiamen.
Just remember what I told you. If I go there and get shot
in the head, just tell them to look for the Utah militia
guys."*

—Ewan's response to a suggestion that the
premiere of *A Life Less Ordinary*
be held in Salt Lake City, Utah

Due to the lengthy three-month shoot to film *A Life Less
Ordinary* and perhaps to keep an eye on her husband after
his public comments about his beautiful costar, Ewan's
wife, Eve, and their daughter, Clara, joined him on location in Utah. During breaks on the movie set, Ewan was
the doting father, proudly carrying Clara in his arms and
singing "doopity-doopity-doo" to her. Eve worked on the
film as a production designer, and the family rented an
apartment in Salt Lake City.

The actor spent his evenings with his family, but on the
weekends he and the film crew partied at a biker bar,
Spanky's, where they played pool and usually got drunk.
Ewan quickly discovered the more beer he consumed, the
better he became on the pool table. On one such night on

the town, Ewan and Diaz sang karaoke in a "redneck" bar without being recognized by the regulars. Ironically, one of the funniest scenes in *My Best Friend's Wedding* was when Julia Roberts tried to embarrass Cameron Diaz's character by forcing her to sing in a karaoke bar.

Even though Ewan and "everyone just had a great time" filming in picturesque Utah, the actor won't be doing any advertisements for the state's tourist department or singing in the Mormon Tabernacle Choir anytime soon. During the three months he spent in the summer of 1996 on location shooting *A Life Less Ordinary,* Ewan never hesitated to express to the press his extreme dislike of the squeaky-clean Mormons who lived in the area. "It was the most conservative, close-minded place I've ever been," he complained. "There's a paranoia and narrow-mindedness here I find terrifying . . . They hated me walking around with my baby because I was a young, scruffy guy . . . And they were really afraid that I might have some fun in my life, that was a huge threat to them. No fun in Utah. It says that when you drive in: 'No fun in Utah. Thank you.'"

Twenty-six-year-old Ewan discovered he couldn't even buy a pack of his favorite smokes, Marlboros, without being carded by convenience-store clerks. But there were many such "weird" experiences while the Scottish film star was on location in Salt Lake City. He told another interviewer: "I've got a black woolen hat and it's got PERVERT written across the front of it. It's the name of the clothing label. And I was with my wife and baby at the supermarket and I didn't think. I just put my hat on Clara's head, because it was cold. And the *looks.* I couldn't figure out why I was getting death looks. And then I realized my ten-month-old baby's wearing a hat with the word PERVERT written on it and these people were like, 'There's Satan out with his kid!' And then I made a point of wearing it every time we went there . . . Maybe they were staring because I only had the one [baby] and I didn't have twelve."

Ewan was not alone in voicing his opinion that Utah was a state too extreme in its religious viewpoints. In early September 1998, after the videocassette version of *Titanic* was released nationwide, employees of Sunrise Family Video in American Fork, a town a few miles south of Salt Lake City, angered one of the movie's distributors, Paramount Pictures, when the video store offered to edit out steamy scenes between the film's stars Leonardo Di-Caprio and Kate Winslet on any purchased copy of the movie. "We will take all necessary and appropriate action to protect our interests," said Dorrit Ragosine, a spokesperson for Paramount Pictures. But Don and Carol Biesinger, who owned Sunrise Family Video, were not intimidated by Paramount's threat of a lawsuit. "The studios have too much power over what people can and cannot see, and that's why we're doing what we're doing at this time," said Don Biesinger, who hoped that video stores in other conservative communities would follow his lead.

"This is a very weird place," director Boyle has added, noting that *Trainspotting* had been banned in Salt Lake City. "Utah's intensely moral and they're desperately concerned about crime, yet there's no morality about business. It's one of just two U.S. states where there's no limit on interest rates you can charge some poor widow who borrows money foolishly, so the morality doesn't extend to the economy."

The citizens of Utah were deeply offended by Ewan and Boyle's critical remarks to the press, but during promotions for *A Life Less Ordinary* a year later, the actor backtracked, "something I've never done before," he said. "I've been quoted as saying the most awful things about Utah, especially in magazines that will be on bookshelves and in shops in Utah right now. And I'm so embarrassed, because I said some flippant, rude things that suddenly came out in print. And how dare I, really? So I'm apologizing to everybody. Because, in fact, they made us feel so welcome there on the whole. We had a really nice time there, and it's a beautiful, beautiful state. However, Salt Lake City is a rather strange town."

One reason that Ewan seemed to have invited problems with the Mormon population while in Utah was his outspoken views on religious faith, especially in a state that is ranked as one of the country's highest in church membership. When one reporter asked, "How do you feel about the topics of the film—love, fate, the heavens?" Ewan responded: "I don't believe in fate in those terms, some other force destining where we go. I think that if there is an idea of destiny, that it is all there [and] all mapped out, then every decision and choice we make is meaningless because it's all going to happen anyway. I think we're incredibly powerful as human beings because we have choice and conscience. It's got to be that way because otherwise I don't want to be part of it. But it's a very nice idea to make a movie about." In another interview at the time, Ewan added to the controversy: "I don't believe someone is pulling all the strings . . . I'd prefer to think that it's up to us, and that there's no higher force."

Ewan almost had to put the Force—the *Star Wars* Force, that is—on hold as the filming for *A Life Less Ordinary* conflicted with George Lucas's production schedule for the first *Star Wars* prequel. "I would have done Danny Boyle's film if push came to shove," the actor later admitted, realizing he would have never become the international star that he is today if he had passed on the opportunity to play the young Obi-Wan Kenobi. "I really love being a part of his [Boyle's] team." Fortunately, filming for the first *Star Wars* prequel was significantly delayed due to Lucas's screenplay rewrites and other problems associated with the sheer size and magnitude of the much-anticipated movie.

"We're lucky to have him," acknowledged producer Macdonald, who is quick to confirm that Ewan should be counted as the fourth member of the dream team. "Tell him to take two steps back, one to the side and do a back flip while singing, and he'll do it three times exactly right. He looks ordinary, but he's magic-looking on camera. No questions, he's part of our core team. It's four of us now."

"It's really exciting to work with them again," Ewan later said. "They're quite unique. They seem to have vision and they seem to know exactly what they want to do. There's always a terrific atmosphere on the set with them, and Danny pushes you in different directions. He's got my full trust, which is very important and he never lets me down."

Specifically, the actor cites Boyle as the best director he has ever worked with. "I've never felt happier working with anyone else," Ewan has admitted in interviews. "He drains your creative juices and makes you work . . . Danny seems to make films the way I feel they should be made. It just makes sense, the way he works. You always have something cool to work for in a scene. You're allowed to create, allowed to work properly as an actor. You can rehearse with him on your own, finding the scene and deciding how to shoot it together, and you come away very satisfied as an actor."

Boyle has been just as complimentary of Ewan. "He has that thing that Jimmy Stewart, his big hero, had. He's not particularly handsome in a conventional way. He could live next to you very easily. But you get him on the screen and he's got the twinkle. The camera loves him . . . He's not into macho roles or looking great. He's prepared to take risks. He loves to show vulnerability and to express emotions. To burst into tears."

"[Robert in *A Life Less Ordinary*] became more interesting as I was playing him," Ewan told a reporter, "because he kind of became more of the feminine character. He's very sensitive, it seems. He reacts and gets very hurt. He's just a guy who gets himself into a terrible mess, and it seems to get worse and worse . . . I tend to be cast as cynical characters, but *A Life Less Ordinary* is a love story, albeit of an odd sort, and I play a sweet, innocent guy. Everything's going a bit weird for him though, and there's more humor in this than anything I've previously done."

Ewan liked nothing more than working with the trio of Boyle (director), Macdonald (producer) and Hodge (writer), but he doesn't think of himself as an essential member of the British filmmaking team. "It's not understood that I'll do all their films," he has stated. "I think what's brilliant about them is their loyalty and their belief in the team. However, the film is all-important and if I wasn't right for a part, I wouldn't be cast in it. I know that the film's more important than their loyalty towards me. And I respect that. That's the way it should be . . . I think after *Shallow Grave, Trainspotting* was a huge risk. I think after *Trainspotting* this is probably a bigger risk."

Trainspotting made more than $60 million worldwide, but it was hoped that that figure would be exceeded by *A Life Less Ordinary.* The critics, however, were less than impressed when the movie was released in October 1997. *USA Today* complained that "Boyle and the gang previously made a movie about shooting junk. Now they've shot one that is junk," adding that *A Life Less Ordinary* "may not be ordinary, but it sure isn't very good." While the *Sydney Morning Herald*'s critic, Sandra Hall, wrote that Ewan "just seems miscast," the *Los Angeles Times* scathingly referred to the film as "a blunder-full life" while stating that "the team that did *Trainspotting* has derailed." The *Milwaukee Journal Sentinel*'s film critic said: "After having trafficked with heroin addicts, the *Trainspotting* team—director Danny Boyle, writer John Hodge, producer Andrew Macdonald and actor Ewan McGregor—have fallen in with really bad company: Hollywood." Noted syndicated film critic Roger Ebert made headlines with "*Trainspotting* Team Makes Ordinary Film" and at the year's end, CNN's reviewer, Paul Tatara (who previously called the movie "completely ordinary") picked the movie as one of the ten worst films of 1997.

"I think it was inevitable that no matter what sort of film these guys made, they were in for a backlash," Ewan later said of Boyle, Macdonald and Hodge. "How do you follow up a movie like *Trainspotting*? To try to make *Trainspotting Part 2* would have been ridiculous, so I think they did the right thing and just went off in a completely different direction ... You can already hear the snidey comments about the film. I think this always happens with number three of anything ... In the end, the people will always decide."

And they certainly did at the box office. In Britain, *A Life Less Ordinary* made millions less than their first movie, *Shallow Grave*. Although in America the film's New York premiere was a star-studded affair with teen heartthrob Leonardo DiCaprio, REM's Michael Stipe, Oasis's Noel Gallagher and Debbie Harry of Blondie in attendance, the box office returns for its opening weekend were not above ordinary at all. It finished in ninth place, taking in a little over $2 million on 1,207 screens, making it the third biggest flop of the year, behind *The Saint* and *Speed 2*.

Although by all accounts, Ewan was disappointed that the romantic comedy didn't capture the hearts of moviegoers as he had hoped, he immediately turned his attention to other acting offers. "It's dreadful," the prolific, hard-working Scotsman told one interviewer. "I guess I am just an actor who can't say no, but every time I try to take a few months off, someone hands me a script that I think is too good to pass up, and I'm running to another film set yet again."

Eleven

EXTREME MEASURES

"I'm so driven—working madly, and almost arrogantly ambitious. But I've never known towards where or what."

—Ewan describing his attitude on filming back-to-back projects

While in the United States filming *A Life Less Ordinary,* Ewan contacted the producers of his favorite television show, *ER,* offering to make himself available as a guest star on America's most popular TV series.

In London, he had already filmed an episode of the long-running horror anthology series *Tales from the Crypt* for the American cable operator HBO. The episode, "Cold War," was directed by Andy Morahan, who also helmed the third installment in the *Highlander* movies. In it Ewan plays Ford, an American whose girl-friend, played by British TV and film star Jane Horrocks, gets involved with another man who is really a vampire. Although Ewan's American accent was a remarkable im-provement over the one he had used in *Nighwatch,* the episode was only shown on cable subscription channels to a limited audience of viewers.

Ewan received a massive amount of exposure, however, when he appeared in the third season of *ER*, a series so popular in the United States that NBC would later pay a groundbreaking $13 million an episode to keep the medical drama on the network's Thursday night lineup of "Must See TV."

In this *ER* episode, "The Long Way Around," Ewan plays Duncan, a hotheaded Scotsman who sets out to rob a Chicago convenience store on Valentine's Day with his American cousin James (Currie Graham). When the shopkeeper fires a weapon at James, his accomplice panics, shoots the owner, and several customers are injured, forcing Duncan to take them as hostages, including Nurse Hathaway (Juliannna Margulies). Although she is finally able to win his trust during the siege, the shopkeeper dies and Duncan is shot by police officers when he attempts to escape from the convenience store. At the end of the episode, Ewan's character dies on the operating table in the hospital's ER.

"The Long Way Around" originally aired in the United States on February 13, 1997, and Ewan earned a prestigious Emmy nomination for Outstanding Guest Appearance on a Drama Series. He lost, however, to *Murder One*'s Pruitt Taylor Vince for his portrayal as the shifty-eyed "street sweeper," a vigilante serial killer of seventeen violent criminals whose prison sentences and plea bargains didn't meet his idea of justice. Ewan's "edgy performance" on the compelling *ER* episode was praised by critics.

The Scottish actor was absolutely thrilled to be appearing on one of his favorite television shows. "I just wanted to be in it, because I love *ER*," he later admitted.

"I got an opportunity to do one and I thought it would be a laugh to see myself in an episode with all the people I'm used to watching in it . . . I've done ten or twelve movies, and when I got the part in *ER,* people went 'You're on *ER!*' "

For an actor with his credentials, it was funny to see Ewan somewhat starstruck on the set of the number-one-rated series. "They are great people," he has said. "They've been doing it for three years together, so they're all quite 'snippy' with each other, not nastily, but their humor is quite personal. George [Clooney] is a very funny guy, though. He never knows his lines. He writes his lines on the beds, you know he is always looking down? He's reading his lines!"

When Ewan was on location in Chicago filming the episode, the die-hard party boy would spend several evenings drinking in the hotel bar. "I'm very, very, very partial to the margarita, it has to be said." The next day on the set, cast and crew members would come up to him and ask in a whisper if he was okay. Ewan emphasized that his alcohol consumption was not unusual in Britain and pointed out that all his friends drank a great deal. "The French drink for pleasure—we just drink."

The actor grows testy, however, if someone tries to lecture him about the ultimate result of drinking too heavily. A huge fan of the legendary British movie and stage star Richard Burton, who died of a brain hemorrhage in 1984, Ewan loves to tell stories about the actor on the sets of his numerous motion pictures: No close-up shots before eleven A.M. (he'd be too drunk), Bloody Marys before the cameras started rolling, and a special post to lean against so he wouldn't lose his balance when he was plastered.

"It's very sad," Ewan has said. "No way do I drink like that. I don't drink spirits [hard liquor], necessarily, and I couldn't handle three or four bottles a day. But it fascinates me because it's extreme, and I like extremes."

"Extreme" is also a word that could be used to describe Ewan's work ethic. When he returned to London after three months away, he had worked for practically two years without taking a vacation. "I'm happiest when I'm working," he has admitted. "I really should take a holiday, I know, but for me there's nothing better than arriving on a film set in the morning and just being someone new. I'm sure I'll be able to work all this out with a therapist in later years, but for now, making movies is just too much fun to stop and think about it."

Ewan reported to work on his next project in March 1997, when he joined the cast of the movie *Velvet Goldmine,* a gay love story set in the early 1970s, during the emergence of the glam-rock scene in London, a time when guys wore stacked heels, fluorescent scarves and eyeliner on stage while screaming songs at the top of their lungs. "I play an American rock 'n' roll star who comes to work in England and meets a sticky end," explained Ewan, who was forced by the film's director to slim down for his role by cutting down on his beer consumption. "I wear lots of long bleached blond wigs, leather trousers and hipster flares. I'm quite grungy. It's the other actors who look high camp. My character isn't based on anyone in particular, but I did watch Iggy Pop videos to get his incredible moves down."

Created by the controversial American independent writer and director Todd Haynes (*Poison, Safe*), and with REM's Michael Stipe as executive producer, *Velvet Gold-*

mine tells the story of Brian Slade, played by up-and-coming Irish actor Jonathan Rhys-Meyes, a fictional David Bowie-like glam-rock star who fakes his own assassination on stage at the height of his fame and disappears from public view. Arthur, an investigative British reporter portrayed by Christian Bale (*The Portrait of a Lady, Little Women*), tracks down Slade's wife, Mandy (Toni Collette of *Emma* and *Muriel's Wedding*). She, in turn, informs Arthur of her husband's sexual fascination with Curt Wild, the American rock star played by Ewan.

Velvet Goldmine (the title of a David Bowie B-side from 1973) was reportedly inspired by the relationship between Bowie and Iggy Pop, and by the rococo world of glitter rock in the early seventies when musicians, especially those in Britain, experimented with gender-bending, outrageous-looking tight pants, women's clothing accessories and sparkly makeup. "What was so interesting about that time," said the film's producer, Christine Vachon, "was that not only was it okay to [experiment] with gender, you had to in order to be musically successful. When you see some old *Top of the Pops* from that time, even bands like the Rolling Stones, who weren't associated with glam-rock, wore lipstick and feather boas. In the end, it went as far as it could. It was almost too dangerous."

"I really love the crazy reversed sexual politics of that era, where being different was the 'in' thing," added Haynes, who won Best Director for *Velvet Goldmine* at the Edinburgh Film Festival in 1998.

Ewan, who spiked his bleached hair like his hero Billy Idol and played in the rock band Scarlet Pride when he was growing up in Crieff, Scotland, was thrilled to live out his teenage fantasies through his on-screen character. "It's the idea of standing there in front of all those thousands of people. It's just you, it's your music, it's not about pretending to be someone else," the actor told reporters. "I don't have the guts but I would love to know what that feels like. It's a fantasy, the rock 'n' roll lifestyle. But because I've got a kid, I'm married and I've got a house, I can't do all that stuff."

In *Velvet Goldmine,* Ewan insisted on actually singing all the songs he performs as Curt Wild in the film instead of lip-syncing as expected. REM's frontman, Michael Stipe, spent an enormous amount of time coaching the actor for the movie's concert scenes. In one particularly elaborate segment, shot in a field south of London at four in the morning, Stipe requested that Ewan go to the extremes for his grand finale. In front of more than two hundred extras, the young actor belted out the end of his musical number while dropping his leather pants to his ankles and exposing himself to the crowd. "I watched a lot of Iggy Pop," Ewan has said. "He's like a small kid, thrashing around in sporadic bursts, not even in time with the music sometimes. It's like he has to let it all out. Having experienced doing that in front of 200 extras, I know that's the key to his character." Ewan later told England's Channel 4 that he had no problem performing nude in *Velvet Goldmine,* but was "uncomfortable" filming the movie's gay sex scenes between his character and his male lover.

"Ewan was very cool about portraying a gay character," director Haynes later said, contradicting Ewan's earlier comments. "When he was doing scenes with Christian [Bale], the two of them would stay in an embrace between takes, and continue to be tender to one another, shutting out the crew. I felt incredible admiration for how secure about their sexuality they were."

After previewing an early screening of the movie, Reuter's news service noted: "McGregor is perfectly brilliant as the charismatic and heroin-addicted Wild, delivering concert performances worthy of the best rock idols." Film critic Janet Maslin also hailed Ewan's "birthday present of a part" after the movie was shown as part of the New York Film Festival in September 1998. Several of Ewan's fans were not so kind, however, accurately predicting that the film would not do well once it was released in theaters worldwide. "People won't get it and will be bored, as there isn't a story to it, really," one online fan posted. "Most of the movie tends to be performance scenes of music videos with tons of voice-overs and flashbacks." Another wrote after previewing the film, "Just don't look too deeply into the movie when it comes time for you to see it. As one friend puts it, 'It's all about imagery and the music.' " A true Ewan fan noted online, however, "There's no way a movie could be bad which features the delectable Ewan sporting long hair and tight velvet pants."

Although director Haynes described *Velvet Goldmine*'s three-month shoot as the "scariest days" of his life, he, too, got into the spirit of the outlandish rock era his movie was attempting to recapture on film. He grew his hair into the style of David Bowie's celebrated Ziggy Stardust character, and dyed it fire-engine red. "I wanted to know what it felt like to wear super-tight skinny little tops that reveal you in ways that haven't been fashionable for men for quite a while now. And it really is a different feeling, being on platform shoes. It's what women experience every day. It was weird."

The movie's cast included the cross-dressing British comedian Eddie Izzard as a rock-band manager, and Brian Molko, lead singer of Placebo (the group that was primarily responsible for a nineties revival of glam-rock) as a member of the New York Dolls, an actual American band. However, the era and its music didn't really appeal to Ewan, who was born in 1971 just as the glam-rock era was getting started. "It's really annoying music, but fashion-wise [such as Tommy Hilfiger's Glam clothing line] . . . there are people wearing more outrageously seventies clothes than we wear in the film. It's a huge statement to make, but I'm not into all that. It seems a bit sad to me."

Ewan has stated repeatedly that he listens to "a massive cross-section of music all the time," but his tastes are much more nineties: "Prodigy, the Chemical Brothers, loads of different stuff," he said. But ever since he heard the first album by Oasis, he has been a huge fan of the popular British rock band. "They're my boys, really." Along with Ewen Bremner (who costarred as Spud in *Trainspotting*), he had the distinct pleasure of announcing Oaisis's performance on the 1996 MTV Video Music Awards. Following the band's appearance on *Saturday Night Live,* Ewan, who was in America filming *A Life Less Ordinary,* stayed out all night partying at a club called Clementine's with band members, teenage heartthrob Leonardo DiCaprio, and half the cast of the NBC hit series *Friends.*

After *Velvet Goldmine*'s eagerly anticipated premiere at the fifty-first annual Cannes Film Festival in May 1998 (where the film's director Todd Haynes won a special award for Best Artistic Contribution), Ewan was cast in the center of a massive record company bidding war between Sony, Virgin and Warner, thanks to his spectacular performance as a rock singer in the movie. Although Ewan sang two songs in *Velvet Goldmine* and at least one on the movie's sound-track album, the actor was surprised that record companies were actually interested in what he considered "a very limited singing voice." The modest Ewan told the *London Times* that when he sang a rendition of the Bobby Darin song "Beyond the Sea" to Cameron Diaz in *A Life Less Ordinary*'s infamous karoke bar scene "it was so embarrassing as Cameron can sing and I can't."

However, Scott Meek, a *Velvet Goldmine* producer, told reporters, "Ewan's voice is great. In fact, it is so good I am sure he will be offered recording contracts." An executive with one of Britain's largest labels admitted that Ewan was his highest-priority signing: "We're prepared to pay over the odds to snap him up," he said. "The British music biz is in need of some new stars at the moment and Ewan is definitely THE man."

Twelve

THE WAN AND OBI

"Including video, I've probably seen it a hundred times."

—Ewan's reply after being told that a recent poll
showed that the average person "felt compelled"
to see the original *Star Wars* 6.7 times

On the first day of filming *Velvet Goldmine* in March 1997, Ewan, dressed in a blond wig, snakeskin pants and platform shoes, was preparing for his first big scene in the glam-rock movie when suddenly his cell phone rang, forcing director Todd Haynes to scream, "Cut!"

On the line was Ewan's agent, Lindy King, who was so excited Ewan could barely make out what she was saying. Finally, the words he had been anxiously waiting to hear for some time came through the phone loud and clear: He was going to play the young Obi-Wan Kenobi in the first installment of the new *Star Wars* prequels in a deal that paid him more than Mark Hamill (Luke Skywalker) and Harrison Ford (Han Solo) had made in the first three *Star Wars* movies combined. "There is no doubt that this movie is the biggest thing that can be," he boasted to reporters, his blue eyes twinkling with excitement.

Just twenty-five-years-old, four years out of drama school, and shooting his sixth film in fifteen months, Ewan seemed to be moving as fast as his character, Mark Renton, down Princes Street during the opening scene of *Trainspotting*.

Morrison's Academy (1985): Ewan, middle row, fifth from left. It was during this time that he pleaded with his parents to allow him to drop out of school and pursue his acting dreams.

Copyright © 1996 by Star Shots Photo Archives, Inc.

Ewan (far right) and his *Shallow Grave* partners-in-crime, Christopher Eccleston and Kerry Fox. To prepare for his character's rude and aggressive behavior in the movie, Ewan listened to tapes of America's Jerky Boys.

Copyright © 1994 by Miramax Films/Star Shots Photo Archives, Inc.

Ewan with two of his *Trainspotting* costars, Robert Carlyle (*The Full Monty*) and Ewen Bremner (*Judge Dredd*). Ewan lost 28 pounds and shaved off his beautiful long hair to look convincing as the film's likable, but self-destructive heroin addict, Mark Renton.

With the release of the new *Star Wars* movie in the summer of 1999, Ewan was at the crossroads of his professional career. The young actor was determined, though, to keep making small-budget, quality films like *Trainspotting*. "I'm not going to stop working and only do that kind of thing [*Star Wars*]," Ewan said. "And whether people remember me for only that film isn't an issue for me because I'll keep doing other work."

In the *Rocky*-like movie *Brassed Off,* Ewan won praise for his intense portrayal of Andy, an unemployed coal miner who keeps his pride and hope afloat by playing in a band. "It's a lovely film," he said, "and I really like the politics of it."

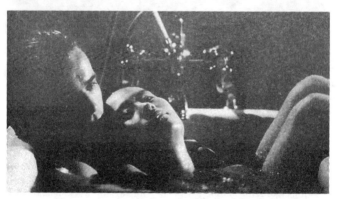

Ewan and his costar Vivian Wu (*The Joy Luck Club*) in a scene from *The Pillow Book,* a movie in which the Scottish actor was nude most of the time. "Usually you'd get arrested for that sort of thing," Ewan said, "but I got paid."

Ewan as *Emma*'s suave, but scheming Frank Churchill. Although the movie was a box office hit, the actor was personally disappointed with his performance and hid under a sofa when he finally watched the film on videocassette.

Ewan and his French wife, Eve (pronounced "Ev"), being mobbed by fans while on-location filming for one of his movies. The young heartthrob knew from the first day he saw her that he had fallen in "marriage-sized love."

Copyright © 1998 by Star Shots Photo Archives, Inc.

Cameron Diaz encouraged rumors of an off-screen romance with her *A Life Less Ordinary* costar, when she stated in interviews to promote the movie: "In the film I fall in love with Ewan's character. And you can see how any girl could fall for him in real life, too. He is an amazing guy, but he's married."

Copyright © 1997 by 20th Century Fox/Star Shots Photo Archives, Inc.

In the first movie he filmed in the U.S., the thriller *Nightwatch,* Ewan played a law school student and part-time security guard who is framed for several murders. Once filming was completed on the movie, Ewan was eager to leave Los Angeles. "A place which destroys you," he said.

Ewan happily poses with one of his fans during a film break from *Eye of the Beholder.* According to a *Glamour* magazine poll, the actor's "cute looks and very Scottish accent" even edged out teen heartthrob Leonardo DiCaprio.

"What I am is an actor, and stardom isn't important to me," Ewan said. "Success is what I strive for, not stardom. I just want to be as good as I can."

After he hung up the cell phone, Ewan lit a Marlboro cigarette to calm his nerves, his jet-black-painted fingernails shaking as the shock slowly wore off and he realized that he was going to be in *Star Wars,* just like his uncle Denis, the relative who had inspired young Ewan to become an actor twenty years earlier. "It was quite a day. I had to walk around knowing I got the part and not being able to tell anyone. It was quite hard," Ewan later said of his frustration of being sworn to secrecy. For the remainder of the day, the consumate professional dove into his *Velvet Goldmine* role, rock star Curt Wild, but when he wasn't filming he walked around the London set in a daze, "and people were saying, 'Are you all right.' And I was like: 'Yeah, fine.' "

Although he wasn't allowed to tell anyone for almost two months that he had won the role of one of the most beloved Jedi ever to tangle with the dark side of the Force, Ewan couldn't keep the news totally to himself. "I told my wife . . . and my parents, and that was it. I didn't tell anyone else for a long while."

The press had been speculating for over a year of Ewan's chances of playing the younger version of Obi-Wan Kenobi, the former Jedi Knight who introduced Luke Skywalker to the Force in the original *Star Wars* movie. However, controversy and name-tossing surrounding the planned prequel kept the guessing game at an all-time high.

The film's casting director, Robin Gurland, had secretly started work on the movie in July 1995, and in the following year she offered Ewan the opportunity for a face-to-face interview. Reportedly, her first impression was that the Scottish actor was perfect for the part of Obi-

Wan, although for almost a year she continued to explore other possible candidates—including Leonardo DiCaprio, Brad Pitt and Kenneth Branagh, the esteemed British actor and star of *Hamlet, Frankenstein* and *The Gingerbread Man,* who would later play Will Smith's archenemy in 1999's *The Wild, Wild West.* However, Branagh and *Star Wars* creator and director George Lucas both claimed that the first time they'd heard about Branagh being considered for the part of Obi-Wan was when they'd read about it in the newspapers.

In an interview by the British magazine *Dreamwatch,* Lucas went on record as stating: "We will have Obi-Wan in the films . . . Over the six films, you'll see him grow from a young Jedi Knight into Alec Guinness [who played the character in the original three movies]. We'll endeavor to mimic the actor with Alec, but there's a quantum leap that you'll have to take—we'll try to make it as subtle a leap as possible. It will not be an American actor, it *will* be a British actor . . . Everything I've read from Kenneth Branagh to Ewan McGregor to a whole lot of stuff—none of it's real."

Referring to rumors of a Ewan screen test for the role of Obi-Wan, *Star Wars* producer Rick McCallum specifically stated in the Dutch periodical *Specifiek Universitair Magazine (SUM)* that although Ewan was a great actor, he had never been screen-tested for the role, which was in direct conflict to what Ewan would later state in interviews to the press: "I met the casting director [Robin Gurland] about a year and half or two years ago. We had a meeting and then, a year later—almost to the day—I went back and met her again. And then I met George [Lucas], and Rick McCallum, who's a producer. Then I screen-tested with Liam Neeson," Ewan said, referring to the star of *Nell, Schindler's List, Rob Roy* and *Les Miserables,* who would play Qui-Gon Jinn, the revered Jedi Master that trains young Obi-Wan in the ways of the Force. "Then I got offered the job. After each audition, I didn't even want to think it could happen. Even now I hate to think about the power of these movies and what I have to do."

Even after Lucas awarded Ewan the role of Obi-Wan, *Star Wars* film production representatives purposely misled the media by stating that a meeting took place between Lucas and Ewan, but that the young Scottish actor was only one of several candidates for the part. Ewan, in response, told several interviewers, "It looks like I'll be playing Obi-Wan," which infuriated Lucas, who wanted to keep casting information about the prequel rolled up tighter than Princess Leia's hair buns.

"With a project this size, they probably don't want to let out anything at all until they're ready to announce the whole cast," said Hollywood casting director Michael Donovan. To make matters worse, the loose-lipped Ewan divulged to *Entertainment Weekly* magazine (in which he appeared on the cover): "What I've been *told* to say, is that we're in negotiations. But the truth is, I want to do it, they want me do it, so I'm doing it."

Finally, *Star Wars* producer Rick McCallum publicly confirmed what everyone had known for several months: "Ewan is playing the young Obi-Wan." Making an admirable attempt at damage control, McCallum continued, "It was very easy to envision him for the role. He can play a variety of roles. If you saw his performance in *Trainspotting, Shallow Grave* and *Emma* you'd see he's like a chameleon. He is really a mercurial, multitalented, multifaceted human being. He just seemed to us the perfect Obi-Wan."

However, in the weeks and months that followed the casting announcement, die-hard *Star Wars* fans expressed their disappointment in Lucas's choice of Ewan as the young Jedi Knight, especially in light of the off-color comments he made to E! Online and other media outlets in which the exhibitionist actor stated that he was hoping there would be a scene in the movie "where Obi-Wan's in the buff. Yeah, when he drops his robes or something and shows everyone his *real* light saber."

Scott Chitwood, a freelance sci-fi magazine writer and a cocreator of one of the best *Star Wars*–related Web sites available on the Internet, TheForce.Net (www.theforce.net/), wrote an online editorial questioning whether Ewan was a suitable role model for young *Star Wars* fans: "So far, he [Ewan] has talked about how he likes to drop his pants and show off his 'lightsaber' in almost every interview he has done. He also ticked off the entire state of Utah with one comment. He describes how he desperately wanted to try drugs in order to better familiarize himself with his role in *Trainspotting*. His speech would probably make a sailor blush and his habits ain't exactly the most healthy you'll run across. Now, of course, that's his own business and he's free to do whatever he wants. But put yourself in Lucas's position. If you're going to be having millions of six-year-olds idolizing him, is this the guy you want?"

For a long time, those type of brutally honest remarks from *Star Wars* fans made Ewan a little nervous. Friends and associates of the actor believe he didn't really comprehend what he had gotten himself into at first. Before it was announced that he would be the new Obi-Wan Kenobi, he had been the star of several offbeat independent British films and hence could say and do what he wanted and nobody really cared. Like Leonardo DiCaprio, who had previously starred in such small-budget movies like *This Boy's Life, What's Eating Gilbert Grape?* and *The Basketball Diaries* before shooting to international superstardom in *Romeo & Juliet* and *Titanic,* Ewan's life was about to be placed under a microscope and billions of people worldwide were going to be watching and listening to everything he said and did. "When I first got the *Star Wars* prequel, I honestly thought, 'Maybe this is not the right thing for me to do,'" Ewan later admitted. "Then I went through a stage where I couldn't even think about it. I was kind of in *Star Wars* denial."

The maverick actor, who always made it publicly known how much he hated big-budget, highly commercialized event movies like *Independence Day,* was about to begin shooting what could possibly become the most commercially successful movie of all time. Still, Ewan saw a difference. "I don't think of the three *Star Wars* movies in the same way I see something like *Independence Day.* I would shoot myself in the head before I was in a film like that," he has admitted. "I think of *Star Wars* movies as being rather unique. I don't see them just as studio blockbusters, in terms of the ideas. I mean, twenty years later, people still want to watch *Star Wars.* I don't think they'll look back on *Independence Day* in the same way, because it's a different kind of thing."

After Ewan confessed that there was no way he could

have said no to George Lucas, one movie critic wrote, "He's not selling out, but he's definitely been upgraded from coach to first class." But the Scottish actor didn't accept the Obi-Wan role so that he could move his career up to that Hollywood A-list of action films. This is *Star Wars,* after all, and it's about fate and destiny. The original installment was the first movie Ewan saw growing up in Crieff, Scotland. His uncle Denis had a minor part in all three of the films, which inspired Ewan to pursue an acting career. But more importantly, now it seemed that his daughter, Clara, would experience the new *Star Wars* installments at almost exactly the same age that he had been when he had experienced the originals. "I remember standing outside waiting to be picked up, so excited," Ewan fondly remembered in several interviews. "And my daughter's going to be six when the new *Star Wars* movies are out. It'll be great for her to have her daddy in it, you know." In fact, Clara will be three when the first installment hits the theaters.

Ewan was just two years old when a young filmmaker named George Lucas first started to work on his classic swashbuckling space epic. The title went through as many changes as the thirteen-page screenplay, evolving from *The Adventures of the Starkiller, Episode One of the Star Wars* to the eventual *Star Wars.* Two Hollywood studios, Universal and United Artists, rejected Lucas's script before an executive at 20th Century-Fox saw its potential to be a blockbuster movie and gambled on it despite opposition from everyone else on the Fox board of directors.

When Lucas would get down on the carpet with his toy airplanes, talk about the Empire, the dark and light sides of the Force and the characteristics of certain Wookiees, even Lucas's friends thought, "George has lost it," according to screenwriter Gloria Katz. "He always had this tunnel vision when it came to his projects, but it seemed like this time he was really out there. 'What's this thing called a Wookiee? What's a Jedi, George?'"

A whole new special-effects factory (Industrial Light & Magic) was constructed to take advantage of new computer technology to implement some of the most elaborate miniature and optical effects ever produced for motion pictures. Lucas and his group of gifted young special-effects wizards created movie magic that had never been seen on the big screen. But it was the strength of a simple but powerful story and the heroics of a handful of colorful characters that actually captured our imaginations and transported us to a galaxy far, far away.

It is now hard to believe that in 1977 the eventual critical and commercial bomb *Exorcist II: The Heretic* was expected to be the biggest box-office hit of the summer. Even 20th Century-Fox was telling movie theaters that if they wanted to show Sidney Sheldon's *The Other Side of Midnight,* they would have to book their science-fiction gamble, *Star Wars.* Film critics shrugged the movie off as a "kiddie" motion picture, a live-action version of a Saturday-morning cartoon. They saw the story of a young farm boy who gets caught up in the middle of a galactic civil war as too simple, with no characterization. Although the film was originally shown on just thirty-two screens, the audience reaction was nothing short of amazing. Across the country, newspapers and radio and television stations reported long lines outside of theaters and snarled traffic jams for most of the summer. In San Francisco the number of people who saw the movie was more than the city's population of 750,000.

Star Wars eventually went on to become one of the biggest moneymaking films of all time. *The Empire Strikes Back* followed in 1980, and three years later *Return of the Jedi* hit movie theaters to close out Lucas's epic three-part tale. With combined worldwide gross ticket sales of $1.3 billion, the three movies comprised the most successful trilogy in movie history. For a limited time at the end of 1995, 20th Century-Fox rereleased the original films as a boxed set of videocassettes to a whole new global audience in thirty-eight countries; more than 9 million units were sold during the first week alone. And in 1997, millions of fans got a chance to watch the special editions of the trilogy when the films returned to movie theaters to celebrate *Star Wars*'s twentieth anniversary. Each film was restored, special effects were digitally enhanced, footage was added, sound was remastered and in the process, a whole new generation of younger fans who had never seen the trilogy on the big screen were introduced to the ways of the Force.

Although a cover story in *Entertainment Weekly* magazine predicted the reworked *Star Wars* would be one of "the biggest gambles of 1997," the first movie alone took in $35.9 million at the box office on its opening weekend, eventually eclipsing *E.T.* as the highest-grossing domestic movie of all time (until *Titanic* broke the record in early 1998). Special video boxed sets later broke yet more records.

Obviously, *Star Wars*' timeless quality had a special effect on movie watchers and, with interest in the trilogy at its highest level since the films were originally released in movie theaters, most moviegoers were wondering whether it would be possible for the next interstellar trilogy—with its first installment planned for the summer of 1999—to live up to the three original classics.

Lucas promised that the new *Star Wars* trilogy would be much more character-driven, substantially complex in dealing with "betrayal among friends," and would center largely on the Jedi Knights, Obi-Wan Kenobi, the collapse of the Old Republic, the rise of the evil Empire, and Anakin Skywalker's transformation into Darth Vader, essentially giving the background for the original three films—what happened *before* Luke Skywalker's adventures.

"I was sort of starting on a little journey with those first *Star Wars* films," Lucas has explained. "Over the last twenty years, I've been able to see the story from a lot of different vantage points and get a lot more depth to it . . . the soap-opera aspect of it, people living their lives and getting into fixes, is the part that's interesting to me."

One thing was certain, however. Once again, there would be hundreds of moviegoers, young and old, standing in line for hours before the first theater showing.

And Ewan McGregor would be starring as the young Obi-Wan Kenobi. "Can you imagine what it'll be like sitting down in some screening room," the actor asked an interviewer, "the curtain goes up and there it is, the new movie? Magic."

No, Ewan, not magic, but the Force, which would be back again.

Thirteen

RETURN TO A GALAXY
FAR, FAR AWAY

*"Actually, I really want to play Princess Leia. Stick some
big pastries on my head. Now, that would be interesting."*

—Ewan joking about his role in
the new *Star Wars* prequel

When filming started on the first *Star Wars* prequel at
Leavesden Studios, just outside of London, in June 1997,
Ewan's uncle, Scottish actor Denis Lawson, joined his
nephew and George Lucas for lunch on the set.

In the canteen there were the cries of "Wedge!" the X-
wing fighter pilot who was the only character apart from
the main cast to survive all three of the original *Star Wars*
films. During the past twenty years, Lawson was constantly amazed at the cult following that had developed
around Wedge Antilles, the number of novels written
about the character and the multitude of Web sites devoted specifically to him on the Internet.

Although the bit parts in the trilogy were just minor
acting credits in Lawson's distinguished movie, TV and
stage career, the sacks of letters, cards and gifts he re-

ceived from die-hard *Star Wars* fans still outweighed all the other mail he received, which was a constant source of irritation to the actor. More annoying, however, was the fact that Lucas was so dissatisfied with Lawson's American accent in the films, the *Star Wars* chief used another actor to dub over his voice.

"They are fantastic films and they are a huge part of cinema culture," Lawson has commented. "As an acting job, for me they were virtually non-existent, almost one of the most insignificant jobs I have ever done. And the fact I get more fan mail for that than anything else is slightly irritating. It is odd, but at the same time it doesn't actually mean very much to me."

Lawson frequently recounts the story of the time he was in a Philadelphia diner with an American actor who proudly informed the two young bartenders that they were serving drinks to Wedge Antilles, Luke's X-wing fighter pilot comrade from the *Star Wars* movies. "They just freaked," Lawson remembered. "I said all I did was fly around and one of them said, 'No man, you changed my life.' I find it very puzzling."

Lawson, who called Ewan's young Obi-Wan Kenobi in the prequels a "major, meaty, and enjoyable role," acted as mentor to his nephew in his early acting career. "Denis helped me with my audition speeches when I started out," Ewan has explained. "He has always been there for me to give advice. His success is partly why I am here. Denis feels a bit silly being associated with *Star Wars*. He's done so many other things but many people know him for that."

Lawson realized his nephew's potential as an actor early on in the young man's life, when he was attending drama school. "Ewan is a different personality to me and I think one of the reasons he succeeds is because he is very self-assured and has a very strong sense of who he is, which he is able to project," he has observed. "It usually takes an actor a few years to find that and he had it right from the word go."

During lunch at Leavesden Studios with Ewan and George Lucas, Lawson admitted that he thought the idea of both he and his nephew appearing in the *Star Wars* universe was almost too strange to be true, "a little bit odd for me, really." When Lucas sat down to eat in the studio canteen, Lawson immediately remarked to his old boss: "George, you're still wearing the same shirt!"

It may have been the same flannel shirt (and jeans and tennis shoes, too) he wore years earlier on the sets of the original *Star Wars* trilogy, but Lucas's attention to detail meant nothing was left to chance in his work. He began composing the first prequel, bearing the working title *The Beginning*, more than three years before actual filming began in the summer of 1997, writing, as always, with number-two pencils, in tiny, compulsively neat-looking script on loose-leaf green-and-blue lined paper clamped in a red binder with LUCAS written in black magic marker on the front. He has written all his scripts in the binder, beginning with *American Graffiti* in the early seventies. Lucas has repeatedly stated that he could probably work faster on his computer but it is superstition that keeps him writing in that binder, just as superstition forced him to wear the same clothes on the massive sets of the new *Star Wars* movie that he had worn on the set twenty years earlier.

The studios used by Lucas and his film crew in Leavesden, England, were easily the biggest motion picture sets in the history of British films. Five hundred construction workers spent months in advance building more than fifty-seven sets on ten stages inside the former Rolls Royce automobile factory. During filming, the full-time shooting crew numbered eighty, but since sets were constantly being built throughout the production, the average number of people who were working in some capacity on the prequel totaled about 350. Almost all of these enthusiastic and energetic crew members were in their late twenties or early thirties, at the beginning of their careers, and grew up watching the original *Star Wars* movies.

If someone was to wander through the studios at Leavesden during the prequel's production, they might have witnessed on one stage the second unit filming green-skinned, multieyed aliens, while on another set they might have watched Lucas directing Ewan as Obi-Wan (costumed in an oversized tunic complete with a three-inch lock of hair for a ponytail) in an important scene with a group of Jedis, including Yoda. In the prop room, a visitor could catch a glimpse of designs for a half-dozen new lightsabers and blasters, while noticing the creature department was filled with familiar faces, some spectacular new ones, and at least one species that had been out pulled out of the background from the *Star Wars* cantina to be given a greater role in the prequel.

No one, however, was going to just happen to wander through Leavesden Studios. Stealing the plans to the Empire's powerful Death Star weapon in the first *Star Wars* movie would have been considerably easier than gaining access to the prequel's production location. Barbed-wire fencing was erected all around the site, and a security checkpoint similar to those used at military installations was set up at the main gate. The chosen few on the movie's set with complete scripts guarded them with their lives, especially after signing confidentiality documents promising not to reveal the contents. Most others got only one or two pages at a time, with no idea how their lines fit into the story line. Well-known actor Samuel L. Jackson (*Pulp Fiction, A Time to Kill, The Negotiator*), who portrays Mace Windu, the revered senior member of the Jedi Council, in the prequel, was sent only six pages of the script, which he received the day before he was to film his scenes. Jackson, who usually has months to spend in preparation for a role, didn't even know who his *Star Wars* character was until he arrived on the set.

According to Terence Stamp (*Superman II, Alien Nation*), who plays the beleaguered Supreme Chancellor Valorum, the paranoia about security reached cosmic proportions on the set of the new *Star Wars* movie: "The wardrobe people have to take Polaroids of you in costume to keep things straight," the actor said in an interview at the time of filming. "Every shot is numbered. If a flash doesn't go off, they have to mark it on a log, so there are no leaks." And although the prequel was officially due to start shooting in September 1997, filming secretly commenced on June 3 to avoid the scrutiny of die-hard fans and the media alike.

Prequel cinematographer David Tattersall told *Entertainment Weekly,* "It's sometimes hard to tell whether they're about to make a movie or launch a military strike. There are guys patrolling the perimeter with dogs and big sticks, and they look mean. You need [computerized] picture IDs and swipe cards to get in everywhere."

George Lucas reportedly produced the *Star Wars* prequel under the alias JAK Productions (named for his children Jett, Amanda and Katie). The title *Red Tails* was used during the early stages of filming, a security tactic similar to the one he used during the making of *Return of the Jedi,* which was dubbed *Blue Harvest,* supposedly the title of a horror movie he was filming to throw curious fans and tabloid reporters off the trail. In addition, when Luke Skywalker told Princess Leia he was her brother, the crew, and even the sound man, were requested not to listen to the exchange of dialogue. Although unusual on other movie sets, such extraordinary levels of secrecy were commonplace on Lucas's sets.

Everyone, from the usually talkative Ewan downwards, was required to sign multipage, iron-clad nondisclosure contracts, agreeing not to speak about the casting or production. When asked by one magazine to comment on the film and its story line after filming was completed, Ewan replied: "I'm not allowed to tell you what the plot is. Are you kidding? You won't hear it from me . . . Nice try, young man, but I'm afraid it's none of your business what Yoda says." Further pestered to discuss the color of his spaceship, Ewan flatly stated, "I'm contractually obligated to ignore you now." Eventually, though, he couldn't resist, and jokingly answered, "Let's just say, I have the sexiest wheels."

After being chastised personally by Lucas regarding his earlier remarks to interviewers about dropping his pants and showing off his "*real* lightsaber" in the new *Star Wars* movie, Ewan told one reporter who relentlessly quizzed him about details of the film's script: "Yeah, right. George wouldn't mind. Actually, he'd cut my tongue out." Months later, the actor admitted to E! Entertainment Television that journalists tried to get him drunk in an effort to learn more about the movie's plot and behind-the-scenes secrets.

Naturally, anything and everything associated with the prequel, especially the casting of characters, became the subject of intense speculation and rumors on the Internet. As Lucasfilm slowly selected the actors for the new *Star Wars* movie, fans were bombarded with erroneous casting reports: *Home Alone*'s Macaulay Culkin was going to play Anakin Skywalker as a child; Kurt Russell was going to portray a young Boba Fett; *Titanic*'s Kate Winslet was rumored to be the young queen, a role that eventually was awarded to Natalie Portman; Harry Connick Jr., the fighter pilot sidekick of Will Smith in *Independence Day,* was allegedly cast as a Jedi Knight; Charlton Heston, who once parted the Red Sea as Moses in *The Ten Commandments,* would either play a Jedi Master or provide the voice of Yoda; and Morgan Freeman (*Seven, Kiss the Girls, Deep Impact*) would be hired for the important role of Qui-Gon Jinn. Before Ewan was cast as young Obi-Wan, there was even an online rumor that Lucas was going to make a mask from digital images of Alec Guinness (the actor who played the older version of the Kenobi in the original *Star Wars* trilogy) in earlier films such as *Lawrence of Arabia,* and then put the mask on the body of an actor who would simply mouth the lines of dialogue from the prequel script. Guinness supposedly would then later dub his voice.

In another uncommon move, the $115 million *Star Wars* prequel was the first movie to have a twenty-four-hour production schedule. Each day, Lucas filmed for twelve hours in Europe, then digitally transmitted the dailies by satellite to Industrial Light & Magic (ILM) in Los Angeles. The company's famous special-effects wizards (numbering between 250 and 400) added the computer-generated images (CGI) of characters, vehicles and even sets into the rough footage overnight, before sending it back to Lucas for his review. By the film's completion, there were over fifteen hundred separate special-effects shots, compared to the meager two hundred in the original *Star Wars* film and far more than the three hundred to four hundred seen in special-effects-laden films such as *Independence Day,* or the almost eight hundred in *Lost in Space.*

Using the latest technology, the *Star Wars* prequel took the art of computer-generated graphics to new levels, creating not only spaceships, but also creature characters and entire planets. Sixty percent of the fifteen hundred special shots utilized CGI, and to accomplish the complicated task of making computer-generated characters act, ILM had to write entirely new software programs. However, prequel producer Rick McCallum was quick to point out that the special effects "only support the story."

From Leavesden Studios in England, filming moved in July 1997 to southern Italy where the cast shot scenes in

La Reggia di Caserta, a national museum better known as the Royal Palace. This majestic building served as the site for an important scene involving the young Naboo queen, played by Natalie Portman (*The Professional, Mars Attacks!, Beautiful Girls*) with outdoor scenes filmed close to the site's waterfalls and gardens. Italian *Star Wars* fans attempted to enter the palace, but were quickly turned away by local police officers and Lucasfilm security personnel.

In late July and August, the production then moved to Tunisia, a small country on the northern coast of Africa, to film the extensive Tatooine desert scenes. Lucas, one of the world's richest men (his entertainment empire is worth an estimated $5 billion) reportedly paid several hundreds of thousands of dollars for a fifteen-mile square section of desert land in Tunisia for the filming of the first prequel. A member of the production crew told a British newspaper: "He [Lucas] bought the land because it means he can blow it up and do whatever he wants on it. He is making three *Star Wars* movies so it's a worthwhile investment."

Although scheduled for a three-week shoot in Tunisia, the production suffered a temporary delay when a freak thunderstorm devastated the outdoor set, which had taken five months to assemble, washing away or outright destroying key pieces of it. The storm, with its torrential rain, sand and winds of up to one hundred miles per hour, was so ferocious that props weighing as much as two tons were thrown the length of a football field, costumes were blown across the desert landscape, alien creatures were half-buried in mud and landspeeders were lifted up like toys and dumped on top of each other. In an eerie coincidence, a similarly devastating storm blew through the original *Star Wars* set twenty years earlier, prompting the superstitious Lucas to view the incident as a surprisingly good omen.

The morning following the storm, everyone rolled up their sleeves and went to work as an enormous clean-up effort was mounted to salvage what was left of the set. Dozens of construction workers were flown in from England, and three hundred extras were reassigned as salvage operators. Surprisingly, filming recommenced at eleven o'clock that morning, just four hours behind schedule. Even the worst-affected sets were back in use within five days. For the following three-and-a-half weeks, Ewan, Liam Neeson (Qui-Gon Jinn), Jake Lloyd (young Anakin Skywalker), the rest of the cast and the 170 members of the prequel's production team toiled in blazing temperatures as they filmed scenes set on the desert planet Tatooine and in the city Mos Espa.

For almost a month, 84,000 bottles of water were drunk; 28,000 packets of rehydrated powder were consumed; 350 tons of equipment were shipped to the Sahara desert film site on eight planes, including the Russian Antonov AN124, the largest transport plane in the world; four cars skidded out of control and tumbled off desert roads; five people almost died of heat exhaustion; and the highest recorded temperature in the shade was 132.8 degrees Fahrenheit.

The secretive Lucas became the hottest, however, when reporters flew over the desert film location in a hot-air balloon and snapped several photos, which later appeared in a German magazine.

Meanwhile, a homesick and exhausted Ewan sought refuge in his desert tent, desperately yearning for the "dreary weather of good ol' London and the gentle tapping of rain against the windowpanes while watching Clara sleep in her bed."

Fourteen

ENDINGS AND BEGINNINGS

"I've really no idea what it's going to look like. An awful lot of the scenes were blue screen shots, where you act to nothing and they put in the effects later on. So I'm probably just as much in the dark about the movie as anyone else."

—Ewan's answer to a reporter who inquired about the new *Star Wars* movie after filming was completed

After three-and-a-half weeks of filming in Tunisia's desert, the film crew returned to England and Leavesden Studios to complete the fourteen-week shoot. Although Ewan spent most of the time "just hanging around" the sets waiting to film his scenes, the boredom didn't really matter. Ewan was living his childhood dreams of being part of the *Star Wars* universe. "Every day I stopped and went, 'Aaaggghhh!' I'm in *Star Wars*!'" Ewan confessed to reporters, putting his hand over his heart.

Because of his uncle Denis's role as Wedge in the original trilogy, Ewan felt like the movies' characters were almost like members of his own family. When he first saw the lovable little droid Artoo-Detoo, the actor almost respectfully bowed to him as if the robot were the king of England. "I walked into the props room and there were about fifty props makers, all of them guys, and I saw R2-D2 at the end of the room. I just started going 'Ahhhh-hhh!!!' All the props makers turned around and they all knew how I felt . . . It certainly is an honor. I went home one day, and my wife was sitting with a lot of mates and I go, 'I worked with R2-D2 today,' and they all looked at me and went 'Who? What?' "

Ian McDiarmid, who played the evil emperor destroyed by Darth Vader in *Return of the Jedi* and who portrays a younger version of the dark overlord as Senator Palpatine in the first *Star Wars* prequel, *really* is like family to Ewan and his uncle Denis. A native of Scotland, McDiarmid was a classmate of Lawson's at the Scottish Academy of Dramatic Arts in Glasgow and the two have remained very close friends over the years. "I met Ewan when he came along to see his uncle and me in a play that we did together, *Volpone,* by Ben Jonson," McDiarmid has said of the new young Obi-Wan. "It wasn't that long ago. He was still in drama school. And like everybody else, I've been delighted to watch his meteoric rise."

Interestingly enough, Kenny Baker, the short actor inside the Artoo-Detoo metal robot outfit, considered Ewan the main source of "fun on the set," and whose free spirit and constant practical jokes "lightened things up considerably and made us not take things so seriously." There was, however, a bit of underlying tension between Ewan and actor Liam Neeson (Qui-Gon Jinn) during filming of the new movie, especially after Neeson told one reporter that Ewan was costarring with him, rather than the other way around, suggesting that he was the prequel's main draw and Ewan was simply a member of the cast.

"A movie set is a huge social occasion for me," Ewan later said. "There's always wonderful, exciting people. You're learning all the time. But I've always found that the actors who try to teach you how to do it are always the ones you don't want to learn from. A lot of older guys do that. 'Oh, sonny, here, this is how you do it.' And I'm always . . . 'That's not how I want to do it.' The people you just *observe* are the ones you learn the most from."

Reportedly, young Natalie Portman, who plays the Naboo queen in the prequel, was another member of the cast whom Ewan found it difficult to work with during filming of the *Star Wars* movie. Although only sixteen years old at the time of the film's production, Portman had previously starred opposite Jean Reno (*Godzilla, Mission Impossible*) and Gary Oldman (*Air Force One, Lost in Space*) in 1994's *The Professional*, playing Mathilda, a young girl who seeks refuge from a hitman after her parents are killed by a corrupt DEA agent. After receiving a Best Actress in Drama nomination for the *Hollywood Reporter* sponsored YoungStar Awards, Portman went on to play a precocious vamp living next door to Timothy Hutton in *Beautiful Girls,* Al Pacino's poorly parented stepdaughter in the crime saga *Heat,* and the president's teenage daughter in *Mars Attacks!* In addition to costarring with Julia Roberts, Goldie Hawn and Drew Barrymore in the Woody Allen old-fashioned musical *Everyone Says I Love You,* the young actress made her Broadway debut in the title role of *The Diary of Anne Frank,* and lent her voice to the $60 million animated film *The Prince of Egypt* in December 1998. According to *Star Wars* cast and crew members, Portman considered herself a movie star who expected everyone to indulge her with almost the same type of royal treatment as her character, the young Naboo queen.

Ewan's favorite cast member (excluding Kenny Baker, the actor inside Artoo-Detoo) was nine-year-old Jake Lloyd, who plays young Anakin Skywalker in the first prequel. The child actor, who also appeared in the films *Jingle All the Way, Unhook the Stars,* thirty television commercials, and like Ewan, guest starred on an episode of *ER,* won the part of the kid who eventually becomes Darth Vader over the six thousand others who auditioned. "I just act like myself," he said at the time of filming. "He's a lot like me. I love doing mechanics, he is one mechanical kid. I like to build stuff, he likes to build stuff. I just act like myself." Jake won praise from Ewan for his "professionalism and talent," but it was the young actor's "masterful handling of a lightsaber" that *really* impressed Ewan. "Jake is just phenomenal."

When asked by one interviewer what he enjoyed most while filming the new *Star Wars* movie, Ewan quickly replied, "The lightsabers! Man, if they were real, they'd be bloody lethal." They almost were for some unlucky production technician who happened to get in the actor's way while he was performing a swashbuckling scene. "The first take and my lightsaber literally flew out of my hands," Ewan later said, admitting that he was a jittery Jedi who dropped his weapon. "No one tells you the sabers have 10-D batteries in them. They burn your hands." When director Lucas yelled, "Action," Ewan screamed and tossed the saber up in the air, hitting a technician in the head.

Ewan's mother, Carol, happily remembered that special afternoon in 1978 when she took her two sons to see their Uncle Denis in the "space adventure called *Star Wars*" at the Odeon movie theater in nearby Perth, Scotland: "The boys just loved it and they both had lightsabers and used them a lot at home. It's really funny to think that Ewan is now using a lightsaber again in the actual film."

"A lot of us used to have to pinch ourselves to remind ourselves what we were involved in," adds Ian McDiarmid. "Ewan, every now and again he'd be holding a lightsaber—'Hey, I'm a holding a lightsaber!' It took him back to when he was a kid, I think."

When a prequel crew member presented Ewan with a padlocked, briefcase-sized wooden box inlaid in black felt with eight or nine lightsaber handles on the first day of filming and asked the actor to choose a color, he picked up "the sexiest one," realizing at that particular moment that he had been waiting twenty years to have his own lightsaber. During rehearsals, the crew burst into laughter as Ewan went through a fight scene mimicking the buzzing sound that a lightsaber made onscreen.

"The first time Ewan and I had to do any lightsaber work," Liam Neeson later said, "we started making the lightsaber noises, and soon felt a bit silly. We kind of looked at each other, [as if] to stop and say, 'Wait, we're professional actors here, we can't be doing this!' "

"There's nothing cooler than being a Jedi Knight," Ewan proudly confessed. "It's so familiar wearing all the Jedi stuff, the clogs and the lightsabers . . . It's part of your childhood, and you're involved in it. It's very weird. The first day I got dressed properly it was a quite a moment for a boy from Scotland to stand there and look in the mirror: 'Jedi McGregor.' "

Nick Gillard, the *Star Wars* prequel's respected stunt coordinator, was especially impressed with Ewan and Neeson, who with little time to prepare for their roles of Obi-Wan Kenobi and his mentor and teacher, Qui-Gon Jinn, quickly mastered the proficient skills of Jedi warriors. "I couldn't have wanted more from either of them," Gillard later acknowledged. "Sometimes they learned ten minutes before we shot a scene. They were that good. I did have more time with Ewan, but he had more complex moves."

At the Leavesden Studios, there was a cart packed full with nothing but lightsabers, waiting on standby. They had been prepared as replacements in the event of damage during Gillard's elaborately choreographed combat scenes, and there were almost a dozen of each fighter's particular design. Long aluminum tubes painted in fluorescent colors would guide the glowing blade effects to be added later by the computer-generated imaging technicians at ILM. Gillard admitted after filming for the prequel was completed: "We've gone through up to 20 of these [lightsabers] a day in action," eventually totaling three hundred of the stunt sabers.

When George Lucas wouldn't allow Ewan to keep his Jedi weapon as a souvenir at the end of the movie's production, the actor expressed his disappointment in several interviews he gave to the media: "I wanted to replace the saber I had as a child with my new one." Although Lucas compared Ewan's performance in the prequel to that of "the perfect young Harrison Ford," who went on to become one of Hollywood's biggest stars after the original trilogy, Ewan was highly critical of his new boss, who was directing his first movie since the original *Star Wars*.

Directors like Danny Boyle (*Shallow Grave, Trainspotting* and *A Life Less Ordinary*) not only allowed Ewan to make suggestions concerning his characters, but actively encouraged the actor to do so. Lucas, who stopped directing films for two decades because "when you're directing, you can't see the whole picture," was blasted by Ewan publicly for telling him "where to stand, what to say, and all that," referring to himself as nothing more than Lucas's puppet. "Most of the time, you're given a mark and told to hit it, deliver some of your dialogue, walk to another over here, and say something else over there." Adding fuel to the fire, the actor also told reporters that Lucas's script dialogue was just plain crap. Ironically, Carrie Fisher, who played Princess Leia, Ewan's favorite *Star Wars* character in the original trilogy, lent her screenwriting talents in an uncredited capacity, to "punch up the dialogue" (as she described it) for the prequel's female characters.

Ewan's criticism was not something Lucas was unaccustomed to hearing. After completion of the original *Star Wars* trilogy, Harrison Ford, who portrayed the smuggler Han Solo in the three previous movies, stated that Lucas had only two directions: "O.K., same thing, only better," and "Faster, more intense." Prequel actor Samuel L. Jackson added that Lucas would simply say at the end of his performances, "Yeah, that was good for me." Even the movie's producer Rick McCallum noted in several interviews that "actual directing was not the most enjoyable process" for Lucas, who much preferred writing and editing his films.

Ewan's biggest grievance was that *Star Wars* actors were only a tiny part of the entire equation of making Lucas's movies. In the grand scheme of things, the actual filming of scenes involving actors was small in comparison to the planned eighteen months of postproduction, when the all-important special effects were added. As a result, Ewan and his fellow actors spent most of their time against a blue screen, the blank canvas upon which the special effects wizards at ILM would later add planets, interstellar vehicles and outer-space battles.

"It was overwhelming the first time George Lucas said, 'Okay, you come in the spaceship, you start it up, and . . .' We were suddenly on the floor, laughing," Ewan has said of his first day of filming on the prequel. "I wondered how you did that. Is there a key? . . . There is a scene [in] which me and Liam are in a cockpit and we have to frown a lot. We spent hours frowning at the camera with some guy speaking into my earpiece telling me to sit in a different position."

Even Neeson acknowledged how difficult it was to pretend to be serious: "The cockpit scenes, I must admit, were very odd," the distinguished actor commented. "When the camera is on me, it's really hard to focus your eyes on something there without having a sort of blank gaze."

"There are two years preproduction, twelve months shooting and eighteen months postproduction," Ewan stated later in interviews. "That shows you how important the acting is. But I never walked into it expecting to give an Oscar-winning performance. I think I did a good job and the film will come out to be absolutely what it was meant to be." Interestingly, Ewan's uncle Denis initially advised his nephew against taking the *Star Wars* rule, warning that he would find the shoot a tedious, technology-bound business.

Despite Ewan's complaints that his acting talents went unchallenged in the movie, everyone associated with the *Star Wars* prequel, including director George Lucas, truly believes that Ewan gave an Academy Award–winning performance in his portrayal of the young Obi-Wan Kenobi, especially in light of the fact that the young Scottish actor was slightly apprehensive about following in Alec Guinness's legendary footsteps. Since he plays a younger version of the same character Guinness portrayed in the original *Star Wars* films, Ewan's preparation included watching the trilogy over and over again, plus several films Guinness made in the 1950s and 60s, including the classic *Lawrence of Arabia,* in which he played King Fiesal.

"Mainly I worked on his voice, really," Ewan explained at the time of the prequel's filming, "trying to take his voice, which is very, very distinct, and put it in a young person's body, which is quite weird. I don't know if it worked or not. Because voice doesn't age very much. There's not that great a difference in the sound of your voice when you're in your 30s or in your 50s." After taking another swig of beer, Ewan cleared his throat, and gave one entertainment-magazine reporter his best Alec Guinness impersonation: "Yoooz the Force, Luke. Stretch out your feeeeeeelings."

Seeking advice and assistance in mastering the actor's voice, Ewan finally went directly to the source: Guinness himself. "There's not a lot of psychological racking around to do here," Ewan recalled the eighty-three-year-old screen legend telling him. "Deliver the lines and hope the background is nicely lit." Guinness later wrote in his 1997 memoir *My Name Escapes Me: The Diary of a Retiring Actor* (in which he briefly mentioned his role in *Star Wars* on only four pages) that twenty years ago he met a child who proudly boasted that he had seen the classic sci-fi trilogy over one hundred times. Guinness told the boy never to see the films again, which made his mother angry because the child started to cry. "Maybe she was right," Guinness said of the woman, "but I just hope the lad, now in his 30s, is not living in a fantasy world of secondhand, childish banalities."

"Sir Alec has done some of the most incredible cinematic acting I have ever seen," Ewan has said with a great deal of respect, "and yet he is a legend for playing Obi-Wan Kenobi . . . To be remembered just as Obi-Wan must be very weird. I think he is still really confused about it himself."

Although Lucas required Guinness and the other original *Star Wars* actors, including Harrison Ford, Mark Hamill and Carrie Fisher, to sign contracts guaranteeing their participation in all three of the original *Star Wars* films, he didn't force any of the first prequel actors to be contractually obligated to appear in the following two movies. During filming of the first film, however, Ewan's agent secured a deal after long and tedious negotiations with Lucas which guaranteed the actor would make approximately $4 million for the second prequel (plus a small percentage of the box-office gross), plus an even higher fee for the third and final movie in the prequel *Star Wars* trilogy.

In addition, Ewan signed a "creative image license,"

which allows him to receive a percentage share of any items that display his physical likeness for the next seven to ten years—no doubt a lucrative deal, considering the fact that *Star Wars* merchandise, such as lightsaber-wielding action figures, stuffed toys, T-shirts, caps, casual wear, outerwear, sweatshirts, childrens' bed sheets and pillow cases, pajamas, lunch boxes, bath towels, posters, book covers, CD-ROMs, calendars, key chains, collector's cards and many, many other items have accounted for several billion dollars in sales.

After wrapping up production on the *Star Wars* prequel at the end of 1997, Ewan, Liam Neeson and Jake Lloyd were scheduled to return to the Sahara desert in Tunisia in January 1998 for additional, or replacement, scenes (better known as "pickup shots") after Lucas reviewed the previously filmed footage. Ewan suffered a severe case of tonsilitis, however, which postponed the movie's reshoots for a couple of weeks. In the summer of 1998, Ewan and other key cast members returned to Tunisia and Leavesden Studios to refilm some last-minute action sequences because George Lucas was reportedly extremely unhappy with several of the movie's scenes. "George is a perfectionist," a film crew member said at the time. "*Star Wars* is his entire life, so he makes sure he gets it right. If he's not happy with the end result for whatever reason, he will do it again, regardless of the costs."

For Ewan, the thrill of the new multimillion dollar movie would not be in the making, but in seeing himself in the completed film. "The exciting thing will be seeing it in the preview theater," he said before its release. "Watching it and seeing what they've put round about you. What wasn't there is suddenly there."

During the various phases of filming the first *Star Wars* prequel, Ewan and the rest of the cast had no idea what the always secretive Lucas was going to call the new movie. Finally, on September 25, 1998, only days after the final reshoots were filmed, the director revealed on the official Lucasfilm Web site that the long-awaited prequel would be titled *Star Wars: Episode I—The Phantom Menace*. Fan reaction was decidedly mixed. "That's a pretty strange title there, George," groused one Web devotee. "It's gonna take some time to get used to this one." Another fan wrote in one of the many *Star Wars* E-mail forums: "It sounds very 'Lucasy' to me. Just look at all the other titles of his films—*A New Hope, The Empire Strikes Back, Return of the Jedi, Raiders of the Lost Ark, The Temple of Doom, The Last Crusade*. I don't particularly like it, but I guess I have to live with it." Other fans were onboard, however: "[It] sounds okay to me, and far better than a lot of the rumored ones, like *Balance of the Force* and *Guardians of the Force*," noted another. Die-hard fans also debated whether or not the film title was a fake. Moviegoers with long memories recalled that Lucas originally announced that 1983's *Return of the Jedi* would be called *Revenge of the Jedi*. "*Phantom Menace* is the title," Lucasfilm's representative Lynne Hale told the press. It was later discovered that Phantom Menace was the name of a villain in the Flash Gordon comics and Lucas titled his new *Star Wars* movie in homage to the sci-fi adventure classic.

Fifteen

ONWARD AND UPWARD

"Things are moving fast for me now, but I'm not worried about losing my head because I already know what I'm doing for the next year."

—Ewan explaining why he didn't have time
to let the *Star Wars* role affect his attitude

When Ewan completed the first phase of filming for the new *Star Wars* movie in late 1997, his face seemingly graced the covers of almost every magazine in the world. "You can't deny it's quite nice seeing yourself," the young actor boasted in interviews. " 'That's me, that's me!' I quite like that."

Ewan's sudden fame suffered a temporary setback, however, in December when *Titanic* opened at theaters and went on to become the biggest blockbuster movie of all time in just a few months, making its star Leonardo DiCaprio the hottest actor around. While Leonardo was breaking hearts *and* box-office records around the globe, Ewan quietly continued to do what he has always done best—work.

Ewan's packed schedule first took him to the seaside town of Scarborough in the northeast of England to begin filming *Little Voice*. Based on the British play *The Rise and Fall of Little Voice* by Jim Cartwright, the film project had been a labor of love for Ewan's friend, director Mark Herman (*Brassed Off*), for quite some time. "That's something I've been involved with for about two years that's now coming into fruition," the actor said during the movie's production. Ewan's decision to commit himself to the film in 1996 had helped Herman secure financial backing for the motion picture from Miramax in America.

Although the nine-week film schedule was planned from the end of October until December 20, 1997, all of Ewan's scenes were shot by mid-November so that the actor could quickly begin work on his next movie and travel to Tunisia for *Star Wars* reshoots. Although his friends were concerned that he was pushing himself too hard and taking on too many film projects, Ewan countered with, "Everyone else works 45 to 50 weeks of the year, so why does it have to be different for an actor?"

Little Voice's big-name cast included well-known movie star Michael Caine, Brenda Blethyn (a 1997 Oscar nominee for *Secrets & Lies*), Jim Broadbent (*The Avengers*), and Jane Horrocks, who appeared with Ewan in the "Cold War" episode of *Tales from the Crypt,* and played the lead role in the original stage version of *Little Voice*. Although the movie's highlight was a star-studded cast, they all agreed to forgo their usual salaries for an opportunity to appear in a project that was dear to director Herman's heart.

In the Cinderella-like story, Horrocks plays Little Voice, a young woman so painfully shy she can communicate only by duplicating the singing voices of legendary songbirds Judy Garland, Billie Holiday and Ella Fitzgerald. Although she becomes romantically involved with telephone engineer Billy (Ewan), triumph quickly turns into tragedy when a conniving, skirt-chasing, has-been agent, Ray Say (Caine), discovers Little Voice and schemes to make a great deal of money from her singing talents.

Before *Little Voice* made its gala premiere at the Toronto International Film Festival in the summer of 1998, one of Ewan's multitude of international fans wrote an anonymous online review after viewing the movie at the first test market screening: "[Ewan] is a minor, but pivotal character. He plays a telephone repairman for the BTT, whose real passion is homing pigeons. He develops a crush on Little Voice because she's sweet and shy, just like him. Little Voice has spent years alone, since her father died, in her room listening to vintage albums. Her mother is a major control freak who never shuts up, thus Little Voice never speaks. But she sings to herself and does dead-on imitations of Judy Garland, Shirley Bassey, and Marilyn Monroe . . . I was floored by her performance. Ewan is rather homely looking in the film (his hair is really dark and poorly combed to the side and his face looks a little pudgy), but he provides the atmosphere for Little Voice to break free, like his homing pigeons. It is a really sweet movie."

Although the cast and crew of *Little Voice* thoroughly enjoyed working with the talented Ewan (producer Elizabeth Karlsen called him "brilliant"), the busy actor moved on to his next movie project before the traditional wrap party at the conclusion of filming in late December. After finishing his scenes for *Little Voice* at midnight on

Sunday, November 17, Ewan was on the set of *Rogue Trader* at London's Pinewood Studios just nine hours later.

Rogue Trader tells the story of thirty-one-year-old Nick Leeson, a crooked high-rolling futures broker based in Singapore, who destroyed London's distinguished Barings Bank in 1995 after he ran up trading losses totaling almost $1 billion. The wheeler-dealer managed to disguise the losses as even larger profits, so at the same time that he was collapsing the bank, he was being congratulated by his employers on his success. After his scheme was discovered, Leeson became a fugitive on the run from law-enforcement agents and was later arrested at the airport in Frankfurt, Germany. The "King of the Exchange," as he was known at Simex, Singapore's international monetary exchange, was returned to Singapore and sentenced to six-and-a-half years in prison for fraud.

The movie, based on Leeson's autobiography of the same name, was written and directed by James Dearden, who had penned the script for the Academy Award-winning thriller *Fatal Attraction*. During *Rogue Trader*'s filming, Dearden's script and direction stressed, even more than the book, Leeson's humble, working-class background and his unlikely rise in the world's oldest merchant bank, Barings, which was founded in 1763. Leeson's suave, sophisticated upper-class English gentlemen bosses at the bank, who gave him free rein, emerge as rather unflattering in the movie. The film's executive producer, British TV interviewer David Frost, suggested that Leeson was the sole scapegoat for the bank's collapse and would not be serving time in prison if he had come from an upper-crust background.

The controversial movie angered many in England because they felt that Leeson, a convicted criminal, was apparently going to profit from his crime. "Nick gets a fee for the rights to his life, all of which will be consumed by the fees for his defense," Frost explained. "Everyone has a right to their life. This is not a violent or sexual crime. It's not a burglary. It's not brutal. It's white-collar crime . . . I came to the conclusion shared by everyone in our crew who met Nick—he absolutely doesn't have a hoard of money stashed away. His lawyers would be furious and disillusioned if that were the case—he could only afford to pay part of their fees."

But does *Rogue Trader* glamorize Leeson? "Well, yeah," admitted Ewan, whose hair was unflatteringly brushed forward for the role. "Though," he added hastily, "I don't think because I'm in it, it's necessarily glamorous. But this film is based on his book, which is bound to glamorize him. You could choose not to make a film based on his book, but that would be a different kind of film."

Of all the people associated with movie, including Ewan, only Dearden visited Leeson in Changi prison in Singapore as part of his research. "He looked unhappy, lonely and isolated," the director/screenwriter said at the time. "He was behind a plate-glass screen, we talked over an inadequate microphone, and 20 people were screaming at the tops of their voices in Chinese and Malay on either side. He was extremely paranoid because he assumed the guards would be listening to our conversation."

Ewan, though, wasn't interested in talking to Leeson about his film portrayal. "What would I say? 'Hi, I'm playing you in a movie, and you're rotting in jail.' It would be awful," the actor later commented. "I don't want to meet him, because I don't want to know what he's like too much. I don't want to have any opinion about him, because people are very black-and-white about the case. Some people think he's a complete animal and some people think that he's a victim. I want to play him in the middle."

After five weeks' shooting at Pinewood Studios, the production set off early in 1998 for mainly exterior scenes in Malaysia, Indonesia and Singapore. Joining Ewan on location was Anna Friel, a popular young actress from the British TV soap opera *Brookside,* who dyed her hair blond to play Leeson's wife, Lisa, in the movie. (Lisa left Singapore with the bank thief, but was not implicated in the scandal, and since returning to Britain has worked as a flight attendant for Virgin Airlines, divorced Leeson, and is set to marry again.) Ewan, who is Scottish, and Friel, who is from Lancashire in the north of England, changed their voices' pitch and tone to speak in the Leesons's London-area accents. Friel felt that the similarities between her and Ewan contributed to their obvious on-screen chemistry: "We are male and female versions of each other. His parents are both teachers; so are mine. His brother flies for the RAF [Britain's Royal Air Force]; so does mine . . . Because of all that, we've given a great performance together. Ewan is the best. He is a wonderful guy."

Off screen, Ewan and Friel became close friends, but rumors and innuendo of an adulterous affair between the couple began when photographs of him kissing his costar appeared in tabloid newspapers back in England. The so-called "scandalous" photos, however, were actually taken during filming of the movie, in which Friel plays Ewan's on-screen wife. Both actors were furious with the press, especially Ewan, who was both disgusted and now suspicious of the newspapers. Thankfully, the unfortunate incident didn't cause any marital problems between the actor and his wife Eve, because friends say their relationship is built on trust and honesty.

Ewan may have taken on better-paying film roles in the twelve months prior to filming *Rogue Trader,* but he enjoyed none of them more—including *Star Wars.* "I feel it's the most acting I've done this year," said the hard-working Ewan. "There's a lot to bite my teeth into."

He read Leeson's autobiography, watched videotapes of David Frost's interview with the criminal on the BBC in 1995 (which was shown in the United States on *60 Minutes*), and had lengthy discussions with two of Leeson's former colleagues from Simex. One of them, Danny Argyopoulos, traded Japanese government bonds on the floor of Singapore's international monetary exchange close to Leeson, with whom he frequently socialized. "Nick was a . . . really nice guy," he said. "I think it's unfair the way he got treated. Barings gave him more than enough rope to hang himself. But I think Nick got carried away with the importance of Barings bestowed on him. They were like, 'you're the king of the exchange.' And he started to believe his own press cuttings."

Ewan has admitted that the pressurized life of being a high-rolling bank trader would never tempt the actor. "I couldn't hack it for five minutes." Yet he hopes to meet Leeson when his prison sentence expires in the year 2001 and after the movie opens: "This was a guy with an intriguing dilemma," noted Ewan. "He started making these massive losses, but what choice did he have but to carry on? The more I learn about him, the more he comes to fascinate me."

In August 1998, however, it was announced that *Rogue Trader*'s early 1999 premiere could be delayed or the script altered after the press reported that the former bank trader was seriously ill with colon cancer. Leeson's attorney in Britain stated that the cancer had spread to his lymph nodes, and with other lawyers, applied for Leeson to be released early from incarceration, citing medical and compassion grounds, so that he could be close to his family who lived north of London (Ewan also told the press that Leeson should be allowed to come back to England). While the rewriting of movie endings is not uncommon, movie industry insiders said the latest twist to Leeson's story would put the filmmakers in a tricky position. "I can't think of a situation like this before," said one.

When Ewan returned home to his family at the end of January 1998, he was physically and mentally exhausted, especially after reshooting several scenes in the blazing Saharan sun of Tunisia for the *Star Wars* movie. Although Ewan felt satisfied professionally, he was extremely disappointed on a personal level. He had been an absentee father who seemingly only saw his young daughter, Clara, when she was sleeping. Finally, after deciding "enough is enough," he organized his schedule so that he could take the entire month of February off to be with his family in London. "I've become tainted by the whole thing. I've pushed my career as far I could," he admitted to British reporters, "but it has become totally mad."

"Ewan absolutely has made his own decisions and knows how to work for himself. And boy does he work," said Ewan's uncle Denis, who noted to the press that the workaholic trait ran in the family. Even at the age of seventy-five, Ewan's grandmother Phyllis was still operating her shop in Crieff, Scotland, in 1998. "She's a human dynamo," Lawson remarked. "Our family is always on the go. Last year, Ewan probably overworked. But he is planning to slow himself up. I would be interested to see if he can do it, though."

Ewan, who doesn't think he necessarily overworks, insisted it was probably time for a change, even though he conceded that the transition was difficult: "I'm still fractious when I get a bit of time on my hands. I get all fidgety."

Sixteen

THE CALM BEFORE
THE STORM

*"I just go about my business and live my life. I've been
in an extraordinary position and I'm very much aware of
the position I'm in life—to be working and have work to
go on to do and to be making films that I feel
passionately about and to be working with very
interesting filmmakers. It's as good as it gets."*

—Ewan's reply after being asked how it felt to
know that his name was a "buzzword" within
the film industry despite only making a
"small amount of movies"

Following in the footsteps of Sean Connery, Bruce Willis,
Michael J. Fox, Jodie Foster, Brad Pitt, Harrison Ford,
Madonna, Sylvester Stallone and a host of other American
and British actors who would never push commercial prod-
ucts in their own countries, Ewan filmed advertisements for
Japanese television. One was for Bobson jeans and the
other for the soft drink Beatnik, short commercials for
which he reportedly made hundreds of thousands of dollars.

Generally, however, Ewan had no interest in self-
promotion, especially on television, claiming that when

American acting legend Robert De Niro appeared on David Letterman's late-night talk show on CBS in the United States, so would he. It was not until 1996 that he was granted his first big interview on British TV, appearing on Chris Evans's *TFI Friday*. During the show, Ewan slipped and said the taboo f-word, and although he apologized immediately, Evans's producers were issued a stiff warning by television censors. "No one can swear like a Scotsman," Ewan jokingly responded to his critics. "It rolls off the tongue so beautifully." However, the actor's father was not amused and asked his son to tone down his foul language in interviews because it embarrassed not only his family, but also the church-going citizens back in his conservative hometown of Crieff, Scotland. In January 1998, Ewan was reluctant to appear on television, and only appeared on Michael Parkinson's talk show after his mother Carol, who had given up her teaching position to become her son's full-time assistant, persuaded him to appear.

Ewan's other television appearances have included dressing up as Minnie Mouse for an Elton John show; presenting Oasis, his favorite band, with an MTV music award; and along with Cameron Diaz, his *A Life Less Ordinary* leading lady, announcing the winner of the Best Kiss at the MTV movie awards in June 1997, an experience he would prefer to forget. "It was stupid and silly," Ewan later complained. "They scripted what we were supposed to say, and it was so awful that we just . . . made up our own thing. We thought we were being really witty, but we were met with this wall of nothing. But, of course, there everyone's just looking around over their shoulders, seeing who's sitting behind them. Everyone's just there to promote something they've been in. Nobody's there just because they want to be."

Although Ewan may have detested self-promotion, others were eager to do it for him. In November 1997, he shot to number one on the British music charts, when the dance group PF Project took a sampling of his voice from the *Trainspotting* sound track for their hit "Choose Life." Ewan heard it for the first time when he was in a Scarborough dance club during the filming of *Little Voice*.

An intensely private young man, Ewan also never boasted of his charitable contributions. He gave support to the Marie Curie Cancer Care and Rachel House children's hospice in Fife, Scotland. After his daughter's almost tragic bout with meningitis ("the worst episode of my life"), he made several secret visits to the hospice to meet with its resident terminally ill children and their families. "Hospices such as the Rachel House do such valuable work, but there's none of the 'poor wee souls' attitude," Ewan has noted. "Instead there is a beautiful atmosphere." With the help of his mother, Ewan also initiated a project that provided voice-overs on movies for the blind; his first endeavor, *Shallow Grave*. In addition, the actor agreed to be the honorary patron by providing funds for the Glasgow Film Theatre, which predominantly showed independent films and encouraged local talent to become involved in the acting profession. Ironically, Ewan's parents were among the founding members of the Crieff Film Society, set up in the early 1970s by a small group of movie lovers to screen noteworthy films in local hotels after the town's theater was permanently closed.

In December 1997, Ewan teamed up with his closest

friends and fellow British actors Jonny Lee Miller, Jude Law, Sadie Frost and Sean Pertwee, plus producers Damon Bryant and Bradley Adams, to form a new $100 million production company called Natural Nylon—the first word representing the group's attitude and the second an acronym for New York and London. Their hopes and dreams were that Natural Nylon would enable them to have more input and control over their work, and provide a way to make innovative international films.

The actors, each with equal shares in the production company, agreed to continue with other work and roles, but promised to devote a substantial amount of their time to Nylon's projects. After announcing that they had secured $100 million funding for ten movies to be made primarily in Britain, even Hollywood took notice, fearing that the company would keep actors like Gary Oldman, Hugh Grant, Daniel Day-Lewis and other leading British actors employed on projects in their native country.

Some members of the Natural Nylon team were scheduled to star in the $23 million David Cronenberg (*Dead Ringers, The Fly*) cyberthriller *eXistenZ* with Jennifer Jason Leigh (*Single White Female, A Thousand Acres*) as a computer programmer who creates a virtual-reality game that taps into the players' minds. Jude Law was also considering a film about the life of the Beatles's manager Brian Epstein, a screen adaptation of Iain Banks's *The Bridge,* and a satirical contemporary thriller based on the book *Psychoville* by Chris Fowler. All five actors were also planning to star in *The Hellfire Club,* a movie set in mid-eighteenth-century British aristocratic society.

Although Ewan had always claimed he wasn't interested in directing, in 1998 it was announced that Ewan and Jude Law would be going behind the camera to film the ninety-minute British television documentary *Tube Tales,* which would combine ten "dramatic, surreal and comic" short stories about real-life experience on the London Underground with a soundtrack by Apollo 440.

In another production partially financed by Natural Nylon, Ewan was scheduled to star in *Nora* as Irish novelist and poet James Joyce, whose literary works aroused both high praise and loud ridicule. Ewan, who had been committed to the project before Nylon was formed, was looking forward to the challenge of "the true nastiness in the man," although the film was more about Joyce's relationship with Nora Barnacle, which according to the actor, was "very sexual and passionate one minute, and so cold, so mean, the next." Ewan was also keen on working with director Pat Murphy: "It's really peculiar I haven't worked with a woman after all the films I've done."

Even though Ewan had been researching Joyce's life in great detail and was anxious to leave for Ireland to begin filming *Nora* ("It's the old great script thing again, really"), he traveled to Montreal, Canada, in spring of 1998 to start work on the $15 million American independent thriller *Eye of the Beholder.* Directed by Australian Stephan Elliot (*The Adventures of Priscilla, Queen of the Desert*), the movie stars Ewan as a high-tech private eye who becomes obsessed with a mysterious woman, played by Ashley Judd (*A Time to Kill, Kiss the Girls*), whom he discovers is a serial killer. Based on the Marc Behm thriller of the same name, the diverse cast also included *Beverly Hills, 90210*'s Jason Priestly and singer k.d. lang. Madonna, who Ewan adored when he was younger, asked to be in the movie, but the Scottish actor exercised his right of cast approval and said no, citing her multitude of trainers and assistants as a possible distraction during filming. "She wasn't very pleased," Ewan later acknowledged, "but there are more interesting people to make movies with."

A major Columbo fan, Ewan wanted to wear a rumpled trench coat and chomp on a cigar as the high-tech detective who is led on a cross-country odyssey by Judd's murderous character. "There's nothing nicer in the afternoon," Ewan has said, "than cuddling up in bed and watching *Columbo*." On the set of *Eye of the Beholder,* Ewan was reportedly very accessible to a group of teenage girls who asked for autographs and their photos taken with the hot young actor. "Ewan isn't like other stars," remarked fan Marie Pier Godère, whose glittered turquoise fingernails caught Ewan's attention. "He's very down to earth." Her only complaint was that he smelled of cigarette smoke from his incessant puffing on Marlboros between the filming of scenes.

Another Montreal fan named Virginia posted her personal impressions on an online bulletin board after meeting Ewan and his fellow acting buddy Jude Law at a pub. "It was a long weekend, a Canadian holiday, so Jude came down to visit him from Toronto, where he is filming *eXistenZ*," she wrote. "Ewan got onstage with the band and sang several classic Irish/Scottish tunes with a guitar, and he also sang U2's 'Running to Stand Still.' He was incredibly gracious when I met him, holding my hand even longer than I dared give it to him!"

Legendary movie star and former Scottish import Sean Connery, with whom Ewan had been compared many times over the past few years, certainly would not con-

sider Ewan "gracious" after the two had a very public disagreement at the opening game for Scotland at the 1998
World Cup soccer match. Connery apparently annoyed
everyone at the party with his ranting about Scottish independence although he hasn't lived in his home country for
several years. The two actors finally got into a war of
words after the former James Bond kept attempting to re-
cruit Ewan for his political cause. Ewan later referred to
the unfortunate uncident as "perhaps inappropriate" after
news of the disagreement was reported by the press: "My
political beliefs have always been my own and I will not
be held up as being against the independence of Scotland," Ewan told reporters. "This situation is rather embarrassing for myself and Sean Connery."

Although he appeared somewhat apologetic about the
disagreement with his fellow Scot, Ewan didn't mince
words a few weeks later when discussing young British
film actress Minnie Driver, who was nominated for an
Academy Award for her role as Matt Damon's girlfriend
in *Good Will Hunting*. During a magazine interview,
Ewan lashed out at Driver, who had decided to relocate
from Britain to Hollywood: "Hello? Minnie? What has
happened to you?" Ewan asked. "Look at her. She's completely reinvented herself. She's gone mad, mad . . . she
wears those little dresses all the time. Ouch, I am so disappointed in her. I can't help it. Why has she bothered
buying into all that rubbish?"

Only days after the remarks about Driver were published, Ewan left for South Africa to film a scene for a U.K.
Comic Relief charity documentary, but was unwittingly
drawn into an armed conflict in the mountain kingdom of
Lesotho (pronounced "Le-soo-too") after an attempted

coup in the region forced the South African government to intervene with military troops. Ewan was supposed to meet comedian Lenny Henry at the top of Sani Pass to act out a scene in which he received a videotape containing a message from Africa. However, six armed border guards rushed Ewan's chartered helicopter when it landed on top of the pass, believing it to be an invading gunship. The pilot said two of the guards searched the chopper thoroughly for weapons despite assurances from Ewan's tour guide that it was "there only for a movie."

After completing the last of the *Star Wars* reshoots at Leavesden Studios in late summer of 1998, Ewan once again stepped away from making movies for a while to spend more time with his family and decided to take a lead role in a stage production. "I've spoken to George Lucas about this at some length," the actor explained, "and he said, 'You have a luxury because you're a British actor. You can do stage, you can go on television, you can do film.' If you're a Hollywood star, if you're an actor my age in L.A., you don't have any luxury with that."

The idea of doing theater work again had originally come to Ewan during the filming of *A Life Less Ordinary* in Utah toward the end of 1996. "I was depressed one night and I phoned my uncle [Denis]," he recalled in interviews. "He's a great ear for me. I said, 'I really want to do a play. I need to do a play before this idea is so frightening I'll never do it again and I want you to direct because I'm frightened enough about it and I think it would be nice if you were there."

The two chose David Halliwell's 1960s farce *Little Malcolm and His Struggle Against the Eunuchs,* better known for its 1974 film version, *Little Malcolm,* which starred John Hurt. Staged at the 174-seat Hampstead Theatre Club, just a short distance from Ewan's home in north London and directed upon request by his uncle Denis, the actor led the cast in sold-out performances from November 18 to December 23 in a tale about art students who rebel against college authorities when they are not allowed to express themselves through their work. Ewan, who was now being paid millions for his film roles, accepted a $418.50-a-week salary to perform in the play.

Although his major stage debut was the "talk of London's theatreland," Ewan had second thoughts beforehand. "It's a dangerous thing for me to contemplate right now," he admitted at the time. "With the British love of building someone up and then tearing them down, I'm setting myself up for some serious abuse. But I really miss the whole process of rehearsing with a bunch of people. And that paralyzing fear of the first night and the adrenalin rush that comes afterwards." For this reason, Ewan said, "I won't be doing Hamlet." Fortunately, *Little Malcom* received positive reviews and later opened at London's Comedy Theatre in the prestigious West End for a limited eight-week run in January 1999. Ewan later said he had hopes of taking the play to Broadway and directing and starring in a new screen adaptation.

Working with his uncle on the play brought back a flood of memories from years earlier when he quit school and began working as a scene-changer at the Perth Repertory Theatre. "I didn't know what acting was," Ewan later recalled. "As far as I knew it was remembering words. And so I was doing a scene for him [Denis] in the school gym, a monologue for an English skinhead, and I was going like this and this [Ewan mimes a series of awkward poses], with no anger. And my uncle stopped me and said, 'Remember when you were beaten up in Glasgow, those guys that punched you in the head, kicked you in the ground, and you looked like a wimp? C'mon, start swearing!'" Immediately Ewan was "standing on the table shouting a blue streak."

After years of discussing the idea, Ewan and his uncle also planned to film in the west of Scotland *Don't Think Twice,* a comedic movie about a struggling rock 'n' roll band, upon the completion of *Little Malcolm and His Struggle Against the Eunuchs* theater run. *Velvet Goldmine, Rogue Trader, Little Voice, Eye of the Beholder* and, of course, the first *Star Wars* prequel were in postproduction and Ewan eagerly awaited the release of the movies in Britain and America throughout 1998 and 1999.

There was also speculation that Ewan was the leading contender in a film version of Iain Banks's psychological thriller *Complicity,* and a starring role opposite his favorite *ER* star, George Clooney, in a movie about prisoners from a Siberian labor camp who walked four thousand miles to freedom. Even Columbia Pictures reportedly wanted Ewan to play John Lennon in Yoko Ono's authorized film version of her romance with the ex-Beatle, who was murdered in 1980 by a deranged fan. However, the movie would likely open old wounds among some fans of the Fab Four, who have long blamed Ono for the British band's breakup. According to the *London Times,* which first reported the story, the movie would attempt to portray Ono as "a peacemaker, soothing tensions between Lennon and [Paul] McCartney in the late sixties, with her trying single-handedly to save the Beatles."

"I was glad to read in the newspapers that I might be

playing John Lennon," Ewan sarcastically remarked. "That would be very nice, but I don't know anything about it. Yoko never got through. Maybe she left a message and I never got it . . . But I'd have to think about that one, because none of the other Beatles would want her to make the film, so I probably wouldn't do it."

Ewan was also linked to a string of other possible movies. In June 1998, *US* magazine asked Boy George to name the actor whom he preferred to play the former cross-dressing Culture Club singer in the film version of his life, *Take It Like a Man.* "Ewan McGregor," he answered. "Although he's prettier than me. Skinnier too. We'd have to feed him some doughnuts." In addition, several publications claimed that Ewan may star as "the evil, illegitimate son of James Bond" in the next 007 movie. *People Daily Online* also reported that *Batman* producer Tim Burton stated he would like to cast Ewan as the villainous Scarecrow in the next installment of the successful movie franchise. Burton said he wanted to replace George Clooney with Kurt Russell as the superhero and Chris O'Donnell (Robin) with Leonardo DiCaprio.

The sought-after young star of *Titanic* was also at the center of one of the few disappointments in Ewan's acting career. Although Ewan had been promised by his longtime friends Danny Boyle, Andrew Macdonald and John Hodge (*Shallow Grave, Trainspotting* and *A Life Less Ordinary*) that he would play the coveted lead role in their film adaptation of Alex Garland's book *The Beach,* the movie production team announced in the summer of 1998 that Hollywood darling DiCaprio would star as the backpacker who discovers a secret cult on a remote island.

Ewan was so desperate to be in the movie that he was

prepared to turn down the *Star Wars* role when, in 1997, it appeared that *The Beach* was going to be filmed at the same time. "*Star Wars* was great fun to do and a very different thing for me," Ewan told one interviewer, "but it's not ultimately what I'm about in terms of an actor in films and stuff. So it was nice that they didn't meet." Ironically, Ewan eventually did turn down the lead role in another Boyle/Macdonald/Hodge film, *Alien Love Triangle,* so that he could star in *The Beach.* British actor Kenneth Branagh (who was supposedly considered for the *Star Wars* role of Obi-Wan Kenobi) was chosen to lead the cast in the sci-fi-oriented movie about a man who discovers that his wife is actually a male alien.

Although *The Beach* was earlier budgeted at $15 million, Boyle and his creative team received $40 million to finance the film from 20th Century-Fox, which included a $20 million paycheck for DiCaprio and funding for the extensive on-location filming in Thailand and Australia. "I was very surprised that they chose Leonardo over me," a heartbroken Ewan said of his former filmmaking buddies, "but it was down to money. They can get a bigger budget with Leonardo. But I thought we were better friends than that . . . There was no big falling-out, but I was hurt. I haven't seen Danny [Boyle] since."

The hurt and bitter feelings of betrayal wouldn't last long, though. For Ewan, superstardom, with its new problems, was just around the corner. Mark Herman, who directed the talented actor in *Brassed Off,* said it best: "Ewan's got the world at his feet, and that makes this a dangerous time for him."

CRYSTAL BALL

"I don't want to walk around going, 'Oh, my God, what's my life going be like after this?' because I'm just going to get on with it."

—Ewan's response after being asked if he was ready for his life to dramatically change after *Star Wars*

"Patrick Stewart, the British actor who plays Captain Jean-Luc Picard in *Star Trek,* has hired bodyguards to protect himself from a psychopathic stalker who has been following him around the world for the past two years. The Shakespearean actor has resorted to such extreme measures, which also include employing private detectives to put the stalker under twenty-four-hour surveillance, to defend himself and his fiancée, Wendy Neuss. . . ."

Ewan glanced one last time at the article in the *London Times* and sighed, wondering if the future would be the same for himself and his family after the international release of the *Star Wars* movie in 1999 and the other two prequels within the first few years of the new millennium. As the new Obi-Wan Kenobi, would he be swarmed by fans every time he rode his Ducati motorcycle down the street to the corner market in London? Would Clara need bodyguards to escort her to school?

Would Eve have to retire from her career as a production designer after being stalked by an insanely jealous female fan? Would they have to buy a new house with high walls and an elaborate security system? Would he and his wife be mobbed when they dined out at restaurants or when he went to have a quiet drink with his buddies at one of his favorite pubs? Worse yet, would Ewan's instant thrust into global superstardom make the young McGregor family prisoners in their own home?

Ewan had always claimed that Hollywood's version of movie stardom didn't interest him, but, in reality, from the moment he accepted the role in the first *Star Wars* prequel, it was no longer something he could ignore. Now he was a household name and his face appeared on children's lunchboxes from Kansas City to Kyoto, Japan. "There's nothing I could do to prepare myself for what might happen," Ewan has admitted. "If that had been a concern, you'd have to think twice about doing the film. It wasn't."

Yet despite all the hype and mass hysteria surrounding *Star Wars,* Ewan was determined to keep making the same type of quality, independent films he had been appearing in for the past decade. "I've done over ten films," the actor told reporters. "There's a body of work behind me. I'm not going to stop making those films. I'm not going to stop working and only do that kind of thing [*Star Wars*] . . . And whether people remember me for only that film isn't an issue for me because I'll keep doing other work."

But just how big a star did Ewan *really* think *Star Wars* would make him? Harrison Ford began his career as the cocky smuggler and rebel hero Han Solo in the original trilogy before going on to become one of the best-known actors of the twentieth century.

"Yeah, look what happened to him," Ewan told one interviewer. "But look what happened to Mark Hamill, though," who had all but disappeared after starring as Luke Skywalker in the three movies. "I suppose it'll all blow over fairly soon and it'll be back to waiting for the phone to ring . . . I still think I'll never work again when a job ends."

And so it seems, thus far at least, there's no reason to worry that the down-to-earth Ewan will turn into some conceited, egotistical star. He remains that likable kid from a small town in the Scottish Highlands who, in the span of ten short years, quit school to pursue an acting career and along the way just happened to become one of the world's biggest stars.

EWAN'S VITAL STATISTICS

Full name: Ewan Gordon McGregor

Nickname: Ew (pronounced "You")

Birthdate: March 31, 1971

Zodiac sign: Sun in Aries, Moon in Gemini

Birthplace: Perth, Scotland

Current residence: London, England

Height: Five foot, ten-and-a-half inches

Weight: Fluctuates depending on acting role, but normally 165

Hair Color: Dirty blond

Eye Color: Blue

Parents' names: James Charles Stewart McGregor (father), Carol Diane McGregor (mother), whose maiden name was Lawson

Brother's name: Colin

Wife's name: Eve (pronounced "Ev") McGregor, whose maiden name was Mavrakis

Daughter's name: Clara Mathilde McGregor

Ewan's nickname for his daughter: Wee lady

Favorite sport(s): Motorcycle racing and soccer

Favorite hobby: Playing golf

Favorite musician: Debbie Harry of Blondie

Favorite band: Oasis

Favorite actor: Jimmy Stewart

Favorite actress: Cameron Diaz

Favorite TV show: *ER*

Favorite drink: Beer, beer, beer

Earliest memory in life: Dropping a Fry's Chocolate Cream bar into the River Earn when he was just two years old and crying uncontrollably about the loss for hours

Favorite childhood memories: Seeing his uncle Denis in *Star Wars* and growing up in the Scottish Highlands where he played knights with his buddies

Favorite cities: London and New York

Favorite movie(s): Jimmy Stewart films and old 1940s and '50s Hollywood romances like *It Happened One Night*

Favorite movie he's made: *Trainspotting*

Musical instrument(s) played: French horn, drums and guitar

Best birthday: His twenty-first, when the cast and crew of the miniseries *Lipstick on Your Collar* presented the new adult with a cake in the shape of a guitar

Little-known fact: When he was five, he used to lip-sync *Hound Dog* and *Don't Be Cruel* while imitating Elvis Presley for his parents and their friends at parties

Best quality: A devoted family man who takes his wife and young daughter to on-location filming of his movies

Worst quality: Smoking, drinking, cursing and speaking before he thinks

Biggest wish: To own a motorcycle racing team

The secret of his success: Drive, ambition and the inability to say "no" when offered acting projects. "The only time I've done work I thought was no good," Ewan has said, "was when I didn't go with my gut instincts."

EWAN FAST FACTS

As a child, his favorite *Star Wars* character was not Luke Skywalker, Han Solo, Obi-Wan Kenobi, or even Wedge Antilles (played by his uncle Denis), but Princess Leia. Ewan has said that he had his first boyhood crush on the actress who played her, Carrie Fisher.

◆

If he were stranded on a desert island and could only be with one person, not including family, Ewan says he would choose his American buddy Terry Haskell: "He was in Vietnam for eighteen months in the jungle, and was shot through the leg. He's one of the funniest men I've ever met, we get on like a house fire."

◆

When Ewan is asked to describe himself, he says he is "slightly arrogant and desperately sincere."

◆

He says people almost never fail to let him down. "I always give—and this isn't just with actors—I always credit people . . . I always assume people are nice people. And I'm just constantly . . . disappointed. Most people aren't."

✦

Politics bore him. "I'm political in such that I'm incredibly aware and passionate about how people are treated," he explains.

✦

After calling *Independence Day* "crap" and repeatedly bashing its star Will Smith in the press, Ewan was worried that the award-winning rap singer and movie star was going to have his bodyguards beat him up at the 1997 MTV Movie Awards.

✦

Ewan is no fan of Hollywood, especially Los Angeles. "I hate it there. All the restaurants are the same. And why is everyone so fat there? It's the land of the fat-free diet, but everyone is huge!"

✦

Ewan roars around the streets of London on his $37,500 Ducati motorcycle.

✦

The actor was featured in the 1998 Pirrelli Tire calendar, the first time a man had been used as a model.

✦

Although his beautiful French wife, Eve, is fashion-conscious, the usually scruffy-looking Ewan (who seldom combs his hair) absolutely hates fashion. "It's a pointless and aimless business," he says.

Ewan was also one of the chosen few in *Select* magazine's one hundred most interesting people. He was ranked number thirty.

◆

Ewan tied with Cameron Diaz and *Titanic* star Kate Winslet at number fifty-six when the *Hollywood Reporter* issued its 1998 Star Power list that ranked four hundred of the world's most bankable stars.

◆

The British edition of *GQ* magazine cited Ewan among its 1998 Men of the Year: "Ewan McGregor is the kind of movie star it's okay to like. A lot."

◆

He confesses that he doesn't feel guilty because he didn't have to struggle for several years, as is the case with most actors. "I didn't get the job to be unemployed and I've learnt from every job I've ever done since."

◆

Ewan still gets a thrill out of working alongside celebrity actors like Robin Williams, Cameron Diaz, Samuel L. Jackson, Nick Nolte and Liam Neeson. "I get excited just going on a film set. Going on location is amazing, hanging about with all these film people doing their thing. If I bump into a star I get all star-struck."

◆

Where will Ewan be in ten years? "I'm not interested in becoming a movie star, but I am very interested in making good movies," he says. "That means to work wherever the script comes from. It doesn't matter whether it's America or wherever. It's good writing that's important to me."

EWAN IN CYBERSPACE

Where do you go on the Internet to find the latest news on Ewan's current and future acting roles, view galleries containing photographs from all his movies, read magazine and newspaper interviews with the Scottish heartthrob, get the latest information on the next installment in the *Star Wars* prequels or communicate online with other die-hard Ewan fans? Here's a list of online websites, E-mailing lists and fan clubs dedicated to Ewan, and to helping inform and inspire new fans.

THE ORIGINAL UNOFFICIAL EWAN MCGREGOR WEB SITE

The *ultimate* Ewan site started out as only one page back in 1996 and has since grown to countless pages featuring over five hundred images.

www.ewanspotting.com

The Ewan McGregor Altar

Cutting-edge features include a message board, animated images, SHOCKWAVE, a mix-and-match Ewan doll, wallpaper for your computer screen and the largest listing of Ewan merchandise on the Internet.

www.beautifulboy.com/ewanmcgregor/

Dante's Ewan McGregor Homepage

A collection of Ewan quotes, photos of the dashing actor, reviews of his television and movie performances, and archives of magazine and newspaper articles are housed at the website devoted to "Ewanites."

www.geocities.com/Hollywood/Academy/4060/

Virtual McGregor

From a Ewan screensaver to cool sound files, check it out!

www.enter.net/~cybernut/ewanmenu.htm

Ewan McGregor Is Amazing!

A fan's Web site dedicated to the "Scottish, talented, and very handsome" actor.

members.tripod.com/~actressMMM/index-2.html

MEGHAN'S HOMEPAGE

A college student's stylish and immense photo gallery showcasing Ewan McGregor's television and movie career.

www.geocities.com/Hollywood/Studio/5252/

THE EWAN MCGREGOR FAN CLUB

When you join the Ewan McGregor online fan club you get the bimonthly *Ewan McGregor Ezine,* an Internet newsletter detailing all the latest Ewan gossip and news.

http://members.aol.com/bluevinyl/clubinfo.html
or E-mail **bluevinyl@aol.com**
Back issues can be found at:
http://member.aol.com/bluevinyl/backissues.html

THE ULTIMATE *STAR WARS* PREQUELS WEB SITE

Catch up on the latest *Star Wars* prequel news, story lines, characters, ships, vehicles and, of course, detailed information on the cast—including the actor who plays the young Obi-Wan Kenobi.

www.theforce.net/prequels

THE EWANSPOTTING E-MAILING LIST FORUM

The Ewanspotting mailing list is an E-mail forum for discussing and exchanging information about your favorite movie star and any related topic. Its purpose is to "connect Ewan fans from all over the world." Subscription to the list is open to everyone and is free of charge. There are two versions of the mailing list available: IN-

STANT form, which means you receive the E-mail posts as they are sent in "real time," and DIGEST form, containing several E-mail posts joined into one big message before being forwarded to you. To join the INSTANT form, simply send an E-mail to:

ewanspotting-request@lists.underworld.net

and in the body of the message, type SUBSCRIBE.

To join the DIGEST form, which will be sent out once a night, send an E-mail to:

ewanspotting-digest-request@lists.underworld.net

and in the message's body, type SUBSCRIBE.

HOW TO CONTACT EWAN

Do you want to tell Ewan you think he's fabulous or get his autograph? Do you want to congratulate or praise him on his performances in his many acting roles? There are numerous ways of forwarding mail to the Scottish heart-throb.

Ewan's official mailing address in the United States is:

Ewan McGregor
c/o Creative Artists Agency (CAA)
9830 Wilshire Blvd.
Beverly Hills, CA 90212-1825

If you live in Europe, write Ewan at the following address:

Ewan McGregor
c/o JAA
27 Floral Street
London

WC2E 9DP
United Kingdom

You can also write Ewan or any of the other *Star Wars* actors in care of the official fan club and the organization will see that your fan mail gets to the person you are writing to:

The Star Wars Fan Club
P.O. Box 111000
Aurora, CO 80042
U.S.A.

Please send a large, self-addressed stamped envelope (SASE) when requesting an autographed picture and be prepared to wait a minimum of eight weeks for a response.

EWAN'S ACTING AWARDS

DINARD FILM FESTIVAL 1994
- Best actor of *Shallow Grave*—award shared with costars Christopher Eccleston and Kerry Fox

EMPIRE AWARDS 1996
- Best Actor

VARIETY CLUB OF GREAT BRITAIN AWARDS 1997
- Best Actor for *Trainspotting*

LONDON CRITICS' CIRCLE FILM AWARDS 1997
- Best Actor for *Trainspotting, Brassed Off* and *Emma*

BAFTA SCOTLAND 1997
- Best Actor for *Trainspotting*

GUILD OF REGIONAL FILM WRITERS 1997
- Robert Shelton Award for outstanding contribution to the British film industry

EVENING STANDARD AWARDS 1997
- Best Actor

SCOTTISH PEOPLE'S FILM FESTIVAL 1997
- Film Personality of the Year

BRITISH FILM INSTITUTE 1997
- Actor of the year—award shared with Sir Ian McKellen

EMPIRE AWARDS 1997
- Best Actor

EMPIRE AWARDS 1998
- Best Actor

NOMINATIONS

MTV MOVIE AWARDS 1997
- Best Breakthrough Performance nomination for *Trainspotting*

EMMY AWARDS 1997
- Best Dramatic Performance by a Guest Actor nomination for *ER*

MTV MOVIE AWARDS 1998
- Best Dance Sequence nomination, with Cameron Diaz, for *A Life Less Ordinary*

FILMOGRAPHY

Being Human (1993)
Tagline: "From the dawn of time man has struggled for just four things: Food. Safety. Someone to love. And a pair of shoes that fit."
Warner Bros.
Directed by: Bill Forsyth
Produced by: Robert F. Colesberry, Steve Norris (associate), David Puttnam
Written by: Bill Forsyth
Costar: Robin Williams, John Turturro, Anna Galiena, Vincent D'Onofrio, Hector Elizondo
Character: Alavarez
Motion Picture Rating: U.S.A., PG-13

Shallow Grave (1994)
Tagline: "What's a little murder among friends?"
Figment Films/Channel Four Films/Glasgow Film Fund/ Gramercy Pictures/PolyGram Filmed Entertainment/ Miramax Films

Directed by: Danny Boyle
Produced by: Andrew Macdonald and Allan Scott (executive)
Written by: John Hodge
Costars: Kerry Fox, Christopher Eccleston
Character: Alex Law
Motion Picture Rating: U.S.A., R; U.K., 18

Blue Juice (1995)
Skreba Films/Channel Four Films
Directed by: Carl Prechezer
Produced by: Simon Relph, Peter Salmi
Written by: Carl Prechezer, Peter Salmi, Tim Veglio
Costars: Sean Pertwee, Catherine Zeta Jones, Steven Mackintosh, Peter Gunn
Character: Dean Raymond
Motion Picture Rating: U.K., 15

Trainspotting (1996)
Tagline: "Choose life. Choose a job. Choose a starter home. Choose dental insurance, leisure wear and matching luggage. Choose your future. But why would anyone want to do a thing like that?"
Figment Films/Channel Four Films/PolyGram Filmed Entertainment/Miramax Films
Directed by: Danny Boyle
Produced by: Christopher Figg (coproducer), Andrew Macdonald
Written by: Irvine Welsh (novel), John Hodge
Costars: Robert Carlyle, Jonny Lee Miller, Ewen Bremner, Kevin McKidd
Character: Mark Renton
Motion Picture Rating: U.S.A., R; U.K., 18

Emma **(1996)**
Tagline: "This summer, Cupid is armed and dangerous."
Haft Entertainment/Matchmaker Films/Miramax Films
Directed by: Douglas McGrath
Produced by: Patrick Cassavetti, Donna Gigliotti (executive), Donna Grey (associate), Steven Haft, Bob Weinstein (executive), Harvey Weinstein (executive)
Written by: Jane Austen (novel), Douglas McGrath
Costars: Gwyneth Paltrow, James Cosmo, Greta Scacchi, Alan Cumming, Toni Collette
Character: Frank Churchill
Motion Picture Rating: U.S.A., PG; U.K., U

Brassed Off **(1996)**
Tagline: "Fed up with the system. Ticked off at the establishment. And mad about . . . each other."
Channel Four Films/Miramax Films
Directed by: Mark Herman
Produced by: Steve Abbott, Olivia Stewart (coproducer)
Written by: Mark Herman
Costars: Pete Postlethwaite, Tara Fitzgerald, Jim Carter, Kenneth Colley, Stephen Tompkinson, Peter Gunn
Character: Andy
Motion Picture Rating: U.S.A., R; U.K., 15

The Pillow Book **(1996)**
Tagline: "Things that make the heart beat faster."
Kasander & Wigman Productions
Directed by: Peter Greenaway
Produced by: Terry Glinwood (executive), Kees Kasander, Jean-Louis Piel (executive), Denis Wigman (executive)
Written by: Peter Greenaway

Costars: Vivian Wu, Yoshi Oida, Ken Ogata
Character: Jerome
Motion Picture Rating: U.S.A., NC-17; U.K., 18

A Life Less Ordinary (1997)

Figment Films/Channel Four Films/PolyGram Filmed Entertainment/20th Century-Fox
Directed by: Danny Boyle
Produced by: Margaret Hilliard (line), Andrew Macdonald
Written by: John Hodge
Costars: Cameron Diaz, Holly Hunter, Delroy Lindo, Ian Holm, Stanley Tucci, Dan Hedaya, Tony Shalhoub
Character: Robert
Motion Picture Rating: U.S.A., R; U.K., 15

The Serpent's Kiss (1997)

Trinity/Berryer Films/Nef/red Parrot/Rose Price Battsek Productions/Miramax Films
Directed by: Philippe Rousselot
Produced by: John Battsek, Hans Brockmann (executive), Francois Duplat (executive), Robert Jones, Tim Rose Price, Tracey Seaward (executive)
Written by: Tim Rose Price
Costars: Pete Postlethwaite, Greta Scacchi, Richard E. Grant, Carmen Chaplin
Character: Meneer Chrome

Nightwatch (1998)

Tagline: "He's the prime suspect in a terrifying mystery. The police are after him and so is the murderer. In the mind of the police, he's the prime suspect. In the eyes of the killer, he's the next victim. What if someone you trusted was setting you up? What if you were the final piece in a brilliant serial killer's puzzle? The night holds the secret."

Michael Obel Productions/Dimension Films

Directed by: Ole Bornedal

Produced by: Daniel Lupi (line), Michael Obel, Bob Weinstein (executive), Harvey Weinstein (executive)

Costars: Nick Nolte, Patricia Arquette, Josh Brolin, Brad Dourif

Character: Martin Belos

Motion Picture Rating: U.S.A., R

Velvet Goldmine (1998)

Tagline: "Style matters. Even when it comes to murder."

Zenith/Single Cell Pictures/Killer Films/Channel Four Films/Goldwyn Films/Newmarket Capital Group/Miramax Films

Directed by: Todd Haynes

Produced by: Christopher Ball (coexecutive), Scott Meek (executive), Sandy Stern (executive), Olivia Stewart (executive), John Michael Stipe (executive), William Tryer (coexecutive), Christine Vachon

Written by: Todd Haynes (also story), James Lyons (story)

Costars: Jonathan Rhys-Myers, Christian Bale, Toni Collette, Eddie Izzard

Character: Curt Wild

Motion Picture Rating: U.S.A., R

Little Voice (1998)

Miramax Films/Scala Productions

Directed by: Mark Herman

Produced by: Laurie Borg (coproducer), Elizabeth

Karlsen, Nik Powell (executive), Paul Webster (executive), Stephen Woolley (executive)

Written by: Jim Cartwright (play), Mark Herman

Costars: Michael Caine, Jane Horrocks, Jim Broadbent, Brenda Blethyn, Annette Badland

Character: Billy

Motion Picture Rating: U.S.A., R

Star Wars: Episode I (1999)

Tagline: "Every generation has a legend. Every journey has a first step. Every saga has a beginning."

20th Century-Fox/Lucasfilm Ltd.

Directed by: George Lucas

Produced by: George Lucas (executive), Rick McCallum

Written by: George Lucas

Costars: Liam Neeson, Natalie Portman, Jake Lloyd, Samuel L. Jackson, Ian McDiarmid, Terence Stamp, Pernilla August, Kenny Baker

Character: Obi-Wan Kenobi

Motion Picture Rating: U.S.A., PG-13

SHORT FILMS

Family Style (1993)
Directed by: Justin Chadwick

Swimming with the Fishes (1996)
Directed by: Justin Chadwick

FORTHCOMING FEATURE-LENGTH FILMS

Rogue Trader
Newmarket Capital/Granada Film Productions
Directed by: James Dearden
Produced by: Claire Chapman (executive), Pippa Cross (executive), Janette Day, James Dearden, David Frost (executive), Paul Raphael
Written by: James Dearden, Nick Leeson (autobiography)
Costars: Anna Friel, Tim McInnerny, Nigel Lindsay
Character: Nick Leeson

Eye of the Beholder
Filmline International, Inc./Hit & Run Productions
Directed by: Stephan Elliott
Produced by: Al Clark (coproducer), Nicolas Clermont, Mark Damon (executive), Hilary Shor (executive), Tony Smith
Written by: Marc Behm (novel), Stephan Elliott
Costars: Ashley Judd, k.d. lang, Patrick Bergin, Genevieve Bujold, Jason Priestly
Character: The Eye (private detective)

TELEVISION APPEARANCES

Lipstick on Your Collar (1993)
Channel Four Films/Whistling Gypsy
Directed by: Renny Rye
Produced by: Alison Barnett (coproducer), Michael Brent (associate), Dennis Potter (executive), Rosemarie Whitman (coproducer)
Written by: Dennis Potter (also story)
Costars: Louise Germaine, Douglas Henshall, Bernard

Hill, Roy Hudd, Kimberly Huffman, Peter Jeffrey, Nicholas Jones, Carrie Leigh
Character: Private Mick Hopper

Scarlet & Black (1993)
British Broadcasting Corporation (BBC)
Directed by: Ben Bolt
Produced by: Rosalind Wolfes
Costars: Alice Krige, Stratford Johns, T.P. McKenna, Rachel Weisz
Character: Julien Sorel

Doggin' Around (1994)
Ariel Productions for BBC
Directed by: Desmond Davis
Produced by: Otto Plaschkes
Written by: Alan Plater
Costars: Elliot Gould, Geraldine James, Alun Armstrong, Liz Smith
Character: Tom Clayton

Kavannagh QC (1995)
Central Films production for ITV
Episode: "Nothing But the Truth"
Directed by: Colin Gregg
Produced by: Chris Kelly
Costars: John Thaw, Geraldine James
Character: David Armstrong

Tales from the Crypt (1996)
Home Box Office (HBO)
Episode: "Cold War"
Directed by: Andy Morahan
Costar: Jane Horrocks
Character: Ford

Karaoke **(1996)**
BBC/Channel Four Films
Directed by: Renny Rye
Costars: Albert Finney, Richard E. Grant, Julie Christie,
Keeley Hawes
Character: Young Man

ER **(1997)**
National Broadcasting Company (NBC)
Episode: "The Long Way Around"
Directed by: Christopher Chulak
Costars: Julianna Margulies, George Clooney, Currie
Graham
Character: Duncan

BIBLIOGRAPHY

Magazines and Newspapers

Abele, Robert. "Ewan McGregor." *US,* April 1997.

Altman, Mark. "The Wars You Never Saw." *Sci-Fi Universe,* July 1994.

Ascher-Walsh, Rebecca and David Hochman. "Fear & Loathing on the Cote d' Azur." *Entertainment Weekly,* 5 June 1998.

Bamigboye, Baz. "McGregor Stages a Surprise." *The Daily Mail,* 6 February 1998.

Billson, Anne. "These Angels Don't Fly." *The Sunday Telegraph,* 26 October 1997.

Boshoff, Alison. "Saturday Premiere in Cannes." *The Daily Telegraph,* 23 May 1998.

Brennan, Judy. "Fox Feels the Force." *Entertainment Weekly,* 17 April 1998.

Brett, Anwar. "Ewan McGregor: Mad About the Boy." *Film Review Special, Year Book 1996/7, #17.*

Carr, Jay. "An 'Ordinary' Romantic Comedy." *Boston Globe,* 24 October 1997.

Chitwood, Scott, Anthony C. Ferrante, Rich Handley, Jenny Peters, Patrick Sauriol, and Matthew Senreich. "Mission Impossible." *Sci-Fi Invasion!,* spring 1998.

"Cinema BigMac from Scotland." *Subway,* January 1998.

Clark, John. "Joined, Hiply." *Los Angeles Times,* 19 October 1997.

Clark, Mike. " 'Emma' and Paltrow: A Sublime Match." *USA Today,* 29 October 1997.

Cohen, Paul B. "Review: Trainspotting." *Magill's Survey of Cinema,* 21 September 1996.

Corliss, Richard. "The Next Brit Bright Star." *Time,* 15 July 1996.

"Countdown to May 25, 1999, STAR WARS: Episode 1." *Cinescape,* July/August 1998.

Crawley, Tony. "*Film Review* at Cannes '98." *Film Review Special #23.*

Daly, Steve, and Gabriele Marcotti. "May the 4th Be With You." *Entertainment Weekly,* 13 June 1997.

Dalton, Stephen. "Canned Heat." *Uncut,* August 1998.

Dawidziak, Mark. "Hit. Miss. Hit. Miss. Hit. Miss." *Akron Beacon Journal,* 23 October 1997.

Dernstein, Robert. "It's a Blunder-full 'Life.' " *Rocky Mountain News,* 24 October 1997.

Dingman, Sarah. "A Life Less Ordinary Is Definitely That." *The Whitworthian,* 11 November 1997.

Dudek, Duane. " 'Life Less Ordinary,' Is Well, Just Ordinary." *Milwaukee Journal Sentinel,* 24 October 1997.

Dwyer, Michael. "A Man of Many Parts." *The Irish Times,* 21 June 1997.

Ebert, Roger. " 'Nightwatch's Review." *Chicago Sun-Times,* 17 April 1998.

Edwards, Gavin. "Ewan McGregor Straight Up." *Details,* November 1997.

Enrico, Dottie. "Dark Side of PepsiCo: Firm Links with 'Star Wars'." *USA Today,* 16 May 1996.

"EW's Guide to the Greatest Achievements and Most Important Records in Show Business History (And Who Can Break Them)." *Entertainment Weekly,* 1 May 1998.

"Face Off: Albert Finney & Ewan McGregor." *People,* 17 November 1997.

Fenster, Bob. " 'Life Less Ordinary' Filmmaker Keeps 'Em Guessing." *The Arizona Republic,* 24 October 1997.

Ferman, Dave. "Bang a Gong! Bring Back Glam." *Ft. Worth Star-Telegram,* 16 May 1998.

Fierman, Daniel. " 'War' Stories." *Entertainment Weekly,* 21-28 August 1998.

———. "Star Wars Watch." *Entertainment Weekly,* 9 October 1998.

Fleming, Michael. "DiCaprio Heads for 'Beach' with Trainspotters." *Variety,* 10 July 1998.

Fredrickson, Anthony. *The World of Star Wars: A Compendium of Fact and Fantasy from Star Wars and The Empire Strikes Back.* Paradise Press, Inc.: Ridgefield, Conn., 1981.

"Future Stars: *Trainspotting*'s Ewan McGregor Opens Up on His *Star Wars* Casting Call." *Cinescape,* July/August 1997.

Gallagher, Gerri. "Mod Couple." *W,* September 1997.

Garner, Jack. "McGregor's Roles Are Varied—And He Likes It Like That." *Gannett News Service,* 24 June 1997.

Gleiberman, Owen. "Skin Flick Peter Greenaway Lightens His Touch in 'The Pillow Book,' an Exotic Tale of the Word Made Flesh." *Entertainment Weekly,* 20 June 1997.

_____. "Trigger Sappy *Trainspotting*'s Creators Aim for an Outlaw Road Romance in 'A Life Less Ordinary,' But It's a Spectacular Misfire." *Entertainment Weekly,* 31 October 1997.

Gordinier, Jeff. "Stupor Heroes From Scotland Comes a Summer Shoot-'Em-Up of a Different Kind." *Entertainment Weekly,* 2 August 1996.

Grant, Steve, "Mr. F***ing Lucky." *Time Out,* November 1998.

Gritten, David. "On a Fast Track." *Los Angeles Times,* 21 July 1996.

_____. "Dealing in Controversy: A Film About Rogue Trader Nick Leeson is Ruffling Feathers—Even Before It's Finished." *Daily Telegraph,* 7 February 1998.

_____. "Trading Places." *Los Angeles Times,* 22 February 1998.

Gross, Edward. "Empire Builder." *Cinescape,* February 1996.

Guinness, Alec. *My Name Escapes Me: The Diary of a Retiring Actor.* Viking Press: New York, NY, 1997.

Harris, Steve, and Chris Kivlehan. "The New Face of Star Wars." *Cinescape Insider, Cinescape Insider, Special Collector's Issue,* August/September 1998.

Hatfield, James, and George "Doc" Burt. *The Ultimate Unauthorized Star Wars Trilogy Trivia Challenge.* Kensington Publishing: New York, NY, 1997.

Heller, Zoë. "A Star's War." *Vanity Fair,* December 1998.

Hirsch, Connie. "Star Wars Turns 20." *Sci-Fi Channel Entertainment,* February 1997.

Hobson, Louis B. "American Arrival." *Calgary Sun,* 13 April 1998.

_____. "Hot Scot." *Calgary Sun,* 26 October 1997.

_____. "McGregor Master of Disguise." *Calgary Sun,* 5 August 1996.

_____. "Old Married Man." *Calgary Sun,* 2 June 1997.

Hofler, Robert. "Lunch with Ewan McGregor." *Miami Herald,* 24 October 1997.

Jacobson, Harlan. "Small Is Big." *USA Today,* 28 August 1998.

_____. "Top Cannes Films Have Ticket to the USA." *USA Today,* 26 May 1998.

Jamieson, Stewart. "Creating the Future." *Starburst,* June 1997.

Jones, Alan. "Ewan McGregor." *Film Review,* November 1997.

Kailich, Isabella. "Ewan McGregor Glams It Up." *Uncut,* November 1998.

Kaplan, David. "The Force Is Still With Him." *Newsweek,* 13 May 1996.

Kardon, Andrew. "Secret Plans." *Sci-Fi Invasion!,* 1997 Special.

Keough, Peter. "Calling All Angels." *Boston Phoenix,* 27 October 1997.

Kerrigan, Jason. "*Trainspotting*'s Ewan McGregor Swings into His Newest Role: *Velvet Goldmine.*" *Talent in Motion,* Summer 1998, Vol. II, Issue 2.

Kirkland, Bruce. "From Junkie to Aristocrat." *Toronto Sun,* 5 August 1996.

Kurtz, Frank. "From Hyperspace to Cyberspace." *Cinescape Insider, Special Collector's Issue,* August/September 1998.

Lane, Randall. "Master of Illusion." *Reader's Digest,* July 1996.

Magid, Ron. "20 Years in the Making." *Cinescape,* March/April 1997.

_____. "The Final Frontier." *Cinescape Insider, Special Collector's Issue,* August/September 1998.

"Many Faces of Star Wars, The." *Cinescape Insider, Special Collector's Issue,* August/September 1998.

Martini, Adriene. "Film & TV: Scanlines." *The Austin Chronicle,* 8 December 1997.

"Master of the Jedi." *Cinescape Insider, Special Collector's Issue,* August/September 1998.

Mathews, Jack. "A Romance Far from Ordinary." *Newsday,* 24 October 1997.

May, Caroline. "Starman: George Lucas and the Reborn Star Wars Trilogy." *Starburst,* March 1997.

McDonnell, David. *Starlog's Science Fiction Heroes and Heroines.* Crescent Books: New York, 1995.

McIntyre, Gina. "Star Tours." *Cinescape Insider, Special Collector's Issue,* August/September 1998.

McKenna, Kristine. "Screwball With an Edge." *Los Angeles Times,* 2 February 1997.

McQuarrie, Ralph. *The Star Wars Portfolio.* Ballantine Books: New York, 1983.

Mosby, John. "Future Wars." *Dreamwatch,* May 1997.

Nashawaty, Chris. "Back to the Future: Twenty Years Later, the Empire Strikes Back." *Entertainment Weekly,* 2 August 1996.

Nathan, Ian. "Caledonian Supernova." *Empire,* November 1997.

Naughton, John. "Now Wash Your Hands." *Empire,* March 1996.

"Neeson Heads '97 Star Wars Cast." *Dreamwatch,* August 1997.

O'Leary, Devin D. "Exquisite Things." *Weekly Alibi,* 11 August 1997.

———. "Heaven and Mirth." *Weekly Alibi,* 4 November 1997.

Parys, Bill. "Ewan McGregor." *US,* August 1996.

Pearlman, Cindy. "Great Scot!" *Cinescape,* January/February 1998.

———. "Star Wars Preview: King of the Desert." *Cinescape,* May/June 1998.

———. "Luscious Jackson." *Cinescape,* July/August 1998.

Pinsker, Beth. "McGregor Doesn't Find Life Ordinary." *The Dallas Morning News,* 25 October 1997.

"Reputations Reassessed: The Heroin Chic of *Trainspotting* is Far From First-Class Entertainment." *Uncut,* August 1998.

"Return to Tunisia." *Dreamwatch,* October 1997.

Richter, Stacey. "Futile Fun: 'Trainspotting' Is Hip and Funny." *Tucson Weekly,* 1–7 August 1996.

Ridley, Jim. "Review: 'A Life Less Ordinary.'" *Nashville Scene,* 3 November 1997.

Rinaldi, Ray Mark. "Mining the Depths of Movie Making: Actor Ewan McGregor Manages to Play Good Guys and Bad Guys With Equal Success." *St. Louis Post-Dispatch,* 5 June 1997.

Rosenthal, Daniel. "A Cast More Extraordinary." *Independent,* 5 October 1997.

Ross, Marion. "Interview With Ewan McGregor." *Film Review,* March 1998.

Sansweet, Stephen. *Star Wars Encyclopedia.* Del Rey Books: New York, 1998.

Sauriol, Patrick. "'Star Wars' Prequels Being Filmed." *Sci-Fi Invasion!,* Fall 1997.

Schwarzbaum, Lisa. "The Late Shift." *Entertainment Weekly,* 24 April 1998.

_____. "Toast of the Coast." *Entertainment Weekly,* 5 June 1998.

Seabrook, John. "Why Is the Force Still with Us?" *The New Yorker,* 6 January 1997.

"Second Childhood." *Starburst,* March 1998.

Seiler, Andy. "The Real Box-Office Champs." *USA Today,* 19 August 1996.

Slavicsek, Bill. *A Guide to the Star Wars Universe* (Second Ed.). Del Rey Books: New York, 1994.

Slavicsek, Bill, and Curtis Smith. *Star Wars Sourcebook.* West End Games: New York, 1987.

Slotek, Jim. "Och, The Force is With Him." *Toronto Sun,* 18 October 1997.

Smith, Caspar Llewellyn. "Yes, I Can Walk and Talk at the Same Time is Cameron Diaz—Star of the Eagerly Awaited 'A Life Less Ordinary.'" *The Daily Telegraph,* 15 October 1997.

"Sneaky Previews." *Cinescape,* July/August 1998.

"Star Wars Episode 1 Confirmed for May '99." *Dreamwatch,* May 1998.

"Star Wars: Episode One Update." *Starburst,* December 1997.

Star Wars Insider, The. Issue #36, February/March 1998.

Star Wars Insider, The. Issue #37, April/May 1998.

Star Wars Insider, The. Issue #37, June/July 1998.

Star Wars Insider, The. Issue #39, August/September 1998.

Star Wars Insider, The. Issue #40, October/November 1998.

Star Wars Insider, The. Issue #41, December/January 1998/1999.

"Star Wars: The Bona Fide Official Line-Up . . ." *SFX Adventures in Science Fiction,* October 1997.

Star Wars: The Movie Trilogy Sourcebook, West End Games: Honesdale, N.Y., 1993.

Stuart, Jan. "Tracking a Meteor from Scotland." *Newsday,* 1 June 1997.

"Summer Movie Preview: The Pillow Book." *Entertainment Weekly,* 16 May 1997.

Svetkey, Benjamin. "It Had to Be Ewan." *Entertainment Weekly,* 13 June 1997.

_____. "The Post Production." *Entertainment Weekly Special: The New Hollywood—Inside the World of Independent Films,* November/December 1997.

_____. "The 'Trainspotting' Trio Sell Out—Sort of—With the

Odd Romance 'A Life Less Ordinary.' " *Entertainment Weekly,* 24 October 1997.

Taylor, Charles. " 'Nightwatch' Boasts All the Trappings That the Quintessential Post-'Seven' Serial Killer Is Wearing This Year." *Salon,* 17 April 1998.

"The It List: The 100 Most Creative People in Entertainment: Ewan McGregor—Star Boy." *Entertainment Weekly* Special Summer Double Issue, 27 June–4 July 1997.

"The It List: The 100 Most Creative People in Entertainment: George Lucas—The Force." *Entertainment Weekly* Special Summer Double Issue, 27 June–4 July 1997.

Thompson, Ben. "Actor Talks to Ben Thompson: Interview with Ewan McGregor." *Independent,* 28 January 1996.

Turan, Kenneth. "A Hellish Match Made in Heaven." *Los Angeles Times,* 24 October 1997.

Vaz, Mark, and Shinji Hata. *From Star Wars to Indiana Jones: The Best of Lucasfilm Archives.* Chronicle Books: San Francisco, Calif., 1994.

Villaneuva, Annabelle. "Musing the Force." *Cinescape Insider, Special Collector's Issue,* August/September 1998.

Vincent, Mal. "The Force Is With Ewan McGregor." *St. Louis Post-Dispatch,* 25 October 1997.

von Busack, Richard. "Banding Together." *Metro,* 29 May–4 June 1997.

Webber, Dan. "Star Wars Lives." *Sci-Fi Universe,* November 1995.

Weiner, Rex. "He's Gotta Have It." *Cinescape Insider, Special Collector's Issue,* August/September 1998.

Willis, John. *Screen World 1997 Film Annual.* Applause: New York, 1998.

Wloszczyna, Susan. "A Life More Than Ordinary Since Trainspotting, McGregor is on the Fast Track." *USA Today,* 24 October 1997.

_____. "Also Opening: 'Nightwatch.' " *USA Today,* 17 April 1998.

_____. " 'Life Less Ordinary' Even Less Noteworthy." *USA Today,* 29 October 1997.

WEB SITES

www.geocities.com/Hollywood/Lot/3419/
www.theforce.net/prequels

www.morrisons.pkc.sch.uk/html/ewan_int.html
www.starwars.com
www.sirstevesguide.com
www.eonline.com/News/Items/0,1,1587,00.html
www.eonline.com/Hot/Qa/Mcgregor/interview3.html
www.eonline.com/Hot/Qa/Mcgregor/interview4.html
www.umagazine.com/launch97/info/entertainment/celeb.html
www3.sympatico.ca/hm/ewan/
www.mrshowbiz.com/news/todays_stories/970811/
    8_11_97_44mcgregor_content.html
www.univercity.com/ewan.html
www.99x.com/noshock/november/ewan.html
www.thei.aust.com/isite/cellrvpillow.html
www.pathfinder.com/people/daily/98back/980619.html
www.december.org/pg/ns/pillow_book/index.htm
www.interlog.com/~funga/Reviews/pillowbk.htm
www.rust.net/mt/oct97/pillow.html
www.tvgen.com/movies/intervus/mcgregor.htm
www.pathfinder.com/altculture/aentries/m/mcgregor.html
www.mmkf.com/official/Trainspotting/3.html
www.echostation.com
www.swalliance.com
www.swdatabase.com/
www.starwarz.com/
www.cinesecrets.com/SW1/pmSW1CastMcgregor.html
www.thehartzs.com/EWAN_MCGREGOR.html
www.prairienet.org/ejahiel/brassed.htm
www.jedinet.com/prequels/casting/ewan.html
www.eonline.com/News/Items/0,1,2789,00.html
www.eonline.com/Hot/Qa/Mcgregor/
www.olivernews.com/wwwboard/star/messages/327.html
www.corona.bc.ca/films/details/sw2.html
www.iftn.ie/cinemas/profiles/ewan.html
www.mediasearch.com.au/archives/cinema_news/nov_todec97/
    life.html
www.worldmedia.fr/cannes96live/cannesva/newsflash/19960513/
    flash015.html
www.filmfestivals.com/cannes96/cfilc16.htm
www.filmscouts.com/reviews/trainsp.html
www.wvgazette.com/Beat/TRAINSPOT.html
www.hollywood.com/movies/life/

www.hotwired.com/movies/96/29/index3a.html
www.thei.aust.com/isite/cellspotting.html
www.uio.no/~christgr/trainsp.html
www.desert.net/tw/08-01-96/cin.htm
www.papermag.com/magazine/trainspotting/indexINFR.html
www1.teletext.co.uk/total/celeb/ewan.htm
www.edstudent.com/inter/ewan_mcgregor.html
www.casenet.com/michael/lifelessordinary.htm
www.tvgen.com/movies/mopic/pictures/39/39616.htm
www.netwiz.net/~robio/trainspotting.html
www.movieweb.com/movie/trainspotting/index.html
www.nj.com/marquee/reviews_new/trainspotting2.html
www.99lives.com/
www.nitrateonline.com/rlordinary.html
www.student.furman.edu/Paladin/1997/11/07/dordinary.htm
www.peak.org/movies/trainspotting.html
www.gl.umbc.edu/~jpeck1/films/lifelessordinary.html
www.shef.ac.uk/~shep/
www.sydney.citysearch.com.au/E/F/Sydne/0000/00/31/
www.sydney.citysearch.com.au/E/E/SYDNE/0000/15/66/cs1.html
www.roughcut.com/whats/alive/life_less_ordinary.html
www.edrive.com/celebs/ewan-mcgregor/bio.html
www.stodgy.com/2b/ewan.html
www2.gol.com/users/zapkdarc/sold23.html
www.celebsite.com/people/ewanmcgregor/index.html
www.pilotonline.com/movies/mv0819emm.html
www.nytimes.com/yr/mo/day/artleisure/01dwye-filmcol.html
www.hotwired.com/movies/95/51/index4a.html
www.hollywood.com/movies/shallow/txtshallow005.html
www.mrshowbiz.com/news/todays_stories/970505/
    5_5_97_mcgregor_content.html
www.mrshowbiz.com/news/todays_stories/970630/
    6_30_97_6ewan_content.html
www.mrshowbiz.com/reviews/moviereviews/movies/65759.html
www.salonmagazine.com/ent/movies/1998/04/17nightwatch.html
www.citysearch7.com/E/M/SFOCA/0000/31/67/cs1.html
www.metroactive.com/papers/metro/05.29.97/
    brassedoff-9722.html
www.christiananswers.net/spotlight/I-brassed.html
www.westword.com/1996/052997/film1.html

www.sacbee.com/leisure/themovieclub2/reviews/archives/
    97bassed/brassed.html
www.eonline.com/Hot/Qa/Mcgregor/interview2.html
www.hebs.scot.nhs.uk/news/drgloc.htm
www.record-mail.co.uk/rm/
www.record-mail.co.uk/rm/features/filmfeat.htm#personality
www.vibes.co.uk/column4.htm
www.smh.com.au/metro/content/961213/cover.html
www.cinema.pgh.pa.us/movie/reviews
www.cinescape.com
cnn.com/SHOWBIZ/9607/trainspotting/index.html
cnn.com/SHOWBIZ/9608/02heroin.chic/index.html
cnn.com/SHOWBIZ/9712/01/review.life.ordinary/index.html
cnn.com/SHOWBIZ/9706/21/review.pillowbook/index.html
cnn.com/SHOWBIZ/9804/20/review.nightwatch/index.html
cnn.com/SHOWBIZ/9705/30/review.brassed.off/index.html
cnn.com/SHOWBIZ/9805/12/cannes/index.html
bigmouth.pathfinder.com/people/movie_reviews/97/pillow.html
us.imdb.com/Name?McGregor,+Ewan
inkpot.com/film/emma.html
weeklywire.com/ww/08-11-97/alibi-film1.html
paddle4.canoe.ca/JamMoviesArtistsM/mcgregor_ewan.html
members.aol.com/bluevinyl/altarhtml.html
movieweb.com/movie/brassedoff/index.html
aristotle.es.twsu.edu/sunflower/ent1.html
cyberwar.com/~smad//general.html
sw.simplenet.com/pages/rumors.html
scifi.simplenet.com/starwars/prequels/episode1.html
scifi.simplenet.com/starwars/prequels/episode2.html
scifi.simplenet.com/starwars/prequels/episode3.html
scifi.simplenet.com/starwars/prequels/cast.html
scifi.simplenet.com/starwars/prequels/general.html
movie-reviews.colossus.net/movies/t/trainspotting.html
books.dreambook.com/romeosdreams/ewan.html
darklords.simplenet.com/ewan1.htm
babelfish.altavista.digital.com/cgi-bin/translate?
homearts.com/depts/pl/movie/07trains.htm
vue.ab.ca/current/fi-mcgre.html
gocinci.net/freetime/movies/mcgurk/life_ordinary.html

Online Interview

Yahoo!, 16 October 1997

Television Interviews

Entertainment Tonight, 6 June 1997
Hollywood Minute, Cable News Network (CNN), 5 June 1997
E! Entertainment Television, 23 September 1998

ABOUT THE AUTHOR

James Hatfield is a syndicated film critic and frequent guest speaker on the sci-fi convention circuit. As the coauthor of *Patrick Stewart: An Unauthorized Biography,* Hatfield won a prestigious international Isaac Asimov Foundation Literary Award in 1997 for Outstanding Biography of an Actor in a Sci-Fi TV Series or Film. He is also the coauthor of several reference/trivia/nitpicking guides to *Star Wars, The X-Files, Star Trek: The Next Generation* and the classic *Lost in Space* television series. Having returned to his native Arkansas from Dallas in 1994, where he was for many years the vice president of a large real estate management company, Hatfield now lives in the Ozark foothills with his wife, Nancy. Most days, the author can be found on the backside of his property, working at his word processor in an old barn-turned-rustic office.

Visit the author's Web site at:

www.omegapublishing.com

or write the author at:

P.O. Box 5453
Bella Vista, AR 72714